SUNNY SIDE-UP

Books by Kathryn Elizabeth Jones

A River of Stones

Parable Series

Conquering Your Goliaths: A Parable of the Five
Stones
Conquering Your Goliaths: Guidebook
The Feast: A Parable of the Ring
The Gift: A Parable of the Key

Marketing Your Book on a Budget

Susan Cramer Mysteries

Scrambled
Sunny Side-Up
Hard Boiled
Over Easy

SUNNY SIDE-UP

A Susan Cramer Mystery

Book 2

KATHRYN ELIZABETH JONES

Idea Creations Press
www.ideacreationspress.com

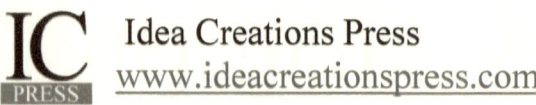 Idea Creations Press
www.ideacreationspress.com

Library of Congress Control Number: 2014916689

ISBN-13: 9780988810730
ISBN-10: 0988810735

Printed in the U.S.A.

Acknowledgments

A big thank you to all of my beta readers and editors. And a huge hug to my number one fan, my husband. Thank you for encouraging me to keep writing - and publishing.

Prologue

The old man wore a black suit, a starched white shirt and a black bow tie, the standard fare for men of his age. They were both on a cruise ship, and though she didn't know him, they'd been speaking. At least, she'd been speaking. The man was drunk and couldn't stand; he'd kept asking her to repeat herself.

She'd been speaking about her divorce and subsequent trip when his blue-gray eyes had clouded over and he'd collapsed in a heap in front of her.

She'd reached for him, of course. But his body had slipped through her fingers like a fish in shallow water. He'd tried to breathe, taking in two shallow gasps. But he was lying there now, his blistered face to the sky, his eyes staring, his left leg bent behind him in some sort of twisted leap. He was dead, Susan was sure of that.

"Help!" she screamed, watching the dance floor for someone, anyone...

And then, as if time had sped up, she was there, an old woman in a gold dress, her bronzed skin twinkling against the burnished fabric. She leaned over the man.

"What happened?" the old woman's voice quivered. It reminded Susan of a child's.

As the salty air caressed Susan's cheeks, she looked out at the great blue ocean. In that moment she thought of Henry.

"I...we were just talking."

The woman in gold, her gray hair perfectly coiffed, reached for the man's wrist. And in that moment Susan saw Henry James as John Middleton, lying dead by the old coal burning stove at the *Hotel Camaro*.

The woman was sobbing, leaning over the man, trying to shake him awake.

"What did you do?" she wailed. Her eyes were a blotchy black and mascara was running down her naked neck.

Susan looked away.

The champagne glass near the deck's railing had spilled. The place where it lodged was a red and sticky, wet.

"I can't wake him!"

The waves must have crashed against the large cruise ship, but Susan hardly noticed; she barely saw those who had suddenly gathered around her including the face of Charles, one of the officers on board ship. He pronounced the man dead.

"But, how can he be…dead?" the old woman gasped, holding her chest, breathing in the sea air in shuddering gasps.

Susan stood next to the railing. She looked out at the sea and wasn't sure when the old man was taken away with his sobbing wife. How had Susan gotten to the railing anyway? Why was the man dead? Had he simply had a heart-attack? Or had someone actually murdered him?

Questions

Susan could see Honolulu in the distance; could almost feel the water, as clear and blue as crystal, feeding her toes. She could almost touch the sand, the small grains of earth keeping her company.

And she could almost see her ex-husband—at least in her mind. She hadn't brought him along, or any other member of her family, naturally, and she hadn't brought along Henry. He'd wanted to come of course, but she had refused.

"I need to do this alone."

"But why? I know it's your dream and all, but you'll be bored without me."

She'd smiled then just as she tried to smile now, but it was no use. The man was dead, and the woman who had come to her aid had found that she'd been leaning over her dead husband. Yes, Susan was one of the suspects.

It was no use thinking about it, but she couldn't help it. It was July 22, her first night on the *Aloha*, the first night of her seven day cruise that she would more than likely be missing. No stroll on Maui, no sea adventure in Hilo, nothing to be experienced in Kona or Kauai. It was Honolulu for one day. Tomorrow was Sunday, and she would probably be taken off the ship in handcuffs.

"So, you want me to come, do you?" She was on the phone and the voice was Henry's. He seemed ecstatic she'd changed her mind.

"Henry, I've been linked to a murder, you've got to come."

"You, what?!" She could see his face going red, though she could only imagine the transition in her mind, his hair combed to either side like the entrails of a fish. "Well?"

She realized she hadn't answered him and it was all she could do from sobbing into the phone. "You've just got to come. I'll be at the Modern Island in Maui, just until they sort everything out."

"And when will that be? You're supposed to be on vacation."

She could hear the frustration in his voice and something else.

"What number can I reach you at?"

"Just call my cell. And Henry?"

"What?"

"Thanks."

***

Susan descended the stairs, tiptoeing at first, and then she traveled more quickly as a faint light coming from the back of the long hall leading to the morgue helped her eyes to adjust. The walls were white and reminded Susan of thick plastic; the floors a sort of dusty gray. The long hallway was lit on either side and sported a metal handrail for support.

The first room held a huge freezer or fridge. What she was sure about were the tall metal racks on either end of the closed-in room and a large fan that whirled slowly as she stepped inside. The walls were metal and the floors appeared to be made out of cement. Food was stacked in bundles, crates and boxes almost to the ceiling and included mostly fish, vegetables and other frozen items that would be cooked up when needed for the guests.

Another section held boxes of wine and beer, even soda, stacked almost to the ceiling. Florescent lighting lit up the boxes. She left the compartment, shut the door, and drew herself further to a dark and cavernous place that held storage for non-perishables. Nothing.

At the end of the long hall, Susan pulled the silver handled door open to reveal another refrigerated compartment—her skin prickled for only a moment, until she discovered the light switch on one wall. This, she turned on. The room was instantly lit, and something else, something Susan could hardly take in.

The dead man's wife was leaning over her husband's intermediary casket; one of three opened metal vaults within a compartmental area. The vaults appeared to be about three feet wide and double that, tall, and were obviously cooled. The 'refrigerator like' breeze chilled her arms.

"Now Joe, you've got to understand why this happened," the woman was saying. She wore a light cream jacket over her gold dress and her hair was no longer beautifully styled.

Susan stood watching. She thought of the late hour. It was near 3 a.m., the light had been turned on, and so far, the woman still hadn't noticed her.

She continued to speak with her dead husband. "You know how life is... I couldn't even talk to the chaplain when he arrived. How could he understand..."

Susan sneezed and the woman's head jerked up, revealing a matted wad of gray hair.

"What are you doing in here?" she spat.

"I...I came..."

The woman scowled. "Do you have any idea who I am?" she asked.

"No," said Susan, feeling the chill on her arms even more here than she had in the food compartment.

"Sylvia. My name is Sylvia and you have made a terrible mistake."

"I just wanted to be sure..."

"What, that you'd killed him sufficiently?" Her body jerked upright and she stood before her, her skeleton-like features reminding Susan of a being half-dead. Her make-up was thick and pancake like, and the tear-filled rivulets flowing down her thin cheeks revealed how much of it had already been washed off. "This was MY husband, you hear?" The sound was like a child's again, and Susan stood like molten rock wondering what she could possibly say.

But she didn't have to say anything. "The chief medical officer said he'd be down here," she sobbed wiping her face with her jacket sleeve. "I hated that Joe would have to be down here all alone. But they told me he would be protected. Protected! As you can see that's mostly a lie. How did *you* get down here?"

Susan didn't know what to say. "Through the doors; I assume, the same as you," she finally offered.

"But there was no guard...no safety officer? You know they have cameras."

"No."

"What about near your room?"

Susan frowned. The safety officer, hired by the ship presumably, had fallen asleep on the other side of her door.

"Then you are fortunate indeed. Perhaps they're all sleeping." She looked down at her husband and this time reached in and straightened his tie. His face was a chalky-blue, the color of an early morning sunrise before the sun peeks over the mountains. He had been fitted with a black suit, and his thin gray hair was slicked back from his face. His thick lips were a chalky-white.

"The medical officer thinks he was poisoned," said Sylvia, brushing back the stray gray tendrils that had fallen from her own face. "What do you know about that?"

"I only know he died in front of me."

"My granddaughter, she's worried. She tells me life on this ship isn't what it should be. What do you think?"

"Do I know your granddaughter?" Susan asked.

The old woman smiled. "No. Help me with the door will you?"

Susan didn't know what to think. All she'd wanted to do was to say she was sorry he'd died, but she couldn't get the words out. Together they shut the door.

***

The ship had docked, it was 8 a.m., and the passengers had been allowed to disembark. She watched the city of Maui from her cabin window. Docked in Kahului Harbor, the sight was impressive. Susan blinked at the tall skyscrapers and watched the airplanes soar overhead. She would miss Kaanapali Beach and the Maui Mall, two of the hotspots she'd been told about in her travel guide.

Instead, she'd have this...

Keith Kealoha was of the islands, and his partner a lovely Ms. Dorothy Levine, with her light hair and blue eyes looked more like a Californian. Each held their badges of gold like a talisman. The interrogation continued. The FBI had already boarded and collected Mr. McLean's body, and Susan was about as dead tired as the man they'd carted off in a gurney. Both cops had evidently spent the night on board ship; both were from the Honolulu Police Department.

Susan tried to maintain her composure. The three of them were in her stateroom and she could feel the breeze off the island's port balcony. She'd chosen a balcony for the same reason she'd brought along a colored bag to gather in the shells—some items a person just had to have.

Kealoha was wearing an officer's uniform, they both were, but he also wore a black and red lei around his thick neck and sported a golden nugget ring on his left forefinger. The woman was attired in a plain gray suit.

"So what do you want to know?" Susan asked.

"Your involvement with Joe McLean."

"Joe?"

"The dead man."

"Oh. There was no involvement. We were both out late and just talking and watching the waves. You know."

"No, I don't know. What sort of connection do you have with Joe?"

"I knew him for about 10 minutes."

Kealoha looked mysteriously over at his partner. Then he turned to her. "What did you talk about?"

"The weather, mostly. And then a bit about his wife."

"What about his wife?"

"Oh, not much. Just that he was glad they'd made the trip—you know, to cruise the islands."

"Did he say anything about being sick?"

"No. It was more, 'I needed some fresh air. You, too?'"

"So you met him out there?"

"No, I was already on deck. He came out and started to talk with me."

"Did you notice anything unusual?"

"Like what?"

"What about the wine he was holding?"

"He must have dropped the glass when he fell. I didn't notice until later that it was by the railing."

"And before that, was he drinking from the glass?"

"I didn't notice."

Kealoha was silent. His partner hadn't yet spoken. Now she said, "So Ms. Cramer, it says here you are divorced."

"Yes, just last year. Why do you ask?"

"No reason, just for the records."

"You say you knew Joe for only 10 minutes. Why would he talk to you?"

"Hmmm, maybe he needed a break from his wife."

"Why do you think he needed a break?" Kealoha again.

"You know how married people are."

"And how might that be, Ms. Cramer?"

A sudden chill raced up Susan's slight back. Even after the heated divorce, which made her feel crazy enough to pretend she had a different sort of life, Susan had maintained her weight as well as her sanity, and when it was all over she'd booked a cruise to the Hawaiian Islands.

She wasn't speaking to her mother or her sister, or fortunately, even her ex-husband Bob, but she was speaking to Henry; she would always be speaking to Henry.

A handshake came next and the two police officers were gone, promising to contact her in a few hours if necessary. In the meantime she was to stay in her stateroom.

Susan got up from the bed and walked to the deck, her bare feet making a slight padding sound as she walked. Lying down on one of the two deck chairs she watched the darkness of the morning sky envelop her. She could hear the waves, smell the sea air and as her eyes closed she thought about the dead man on deck.

He was dead...dead! And it was like the *Hotel Camaro* incident all over again! How difficult it had been to leave that place with all of her duties, but with Henry's help, and the quick thinking of her new assistant Ms. Jane Dove, Susan had been able to leave for the 7 day cruise. It had been three years, and the trip was long overdue. And now this!

As Susan reflected on what had occurred she might have slept: the time was near 10 a.m. but she wasn't hungry either.

The body had been taken away, more than likely with his wife. But what about Mrs. McLean's room? Perhaps the police had missed some well-needed evidence. But she couldn't go anywhere. The police stood guard at her door, and before long, they'd be taking her away from here. Where was Henry? How long would she have to wait for him?

SUNNY SIDE-UP

Early Morning Visit

It was Monday, the third night of her cruise. The ship was still docked in Maui and would be leaving by 6 p.m. Henry hadn't come for her, and the police were still surveying the damage. And then it came.

She was in bed when she heard a bang on her door. Susan looked at the clock. It was 3:30 p.m. She'd overslept by a long shot and hadn't had breakfast or lunch. Susan got up and answered the door, wondering if the police would finally be letting her go. Maybe she'd be able to continue to Hilo after all.

But it was only one of the stewards. The pin said, *Jacob*. "I've come for you, ma'am," he said, wiping at his short hair and bending a little at the knees. He was probably 19.

"Now?" She looked up and down the hall for the police but could see no one.

"Sorry, but we need to talk before you leave the ship," he said.

"I'm not even dressed."

"I'll wait—out here," he added. He pointed to the red carpeted hall, just one of the many carpet colors in the cruise ship, which helped passengers more easily locate their cabin room.

Susan showered quickly, dressed, and gathered the few supplies she hadn't yet put back into her suitcase. There wasn't time to put on make-up or do her hair. Jacob, she couldn't have him standing on the other side of her door forever.

With everything gathered she reached for the door and walked out. Sure enough, he was still standing there, looking at nothing in particular, his left leg bouncing to some jingle he knew in his head.

"Do I bring this?" She showed him her suitcase. It was old and sported flowers—an embarrassment, but the only traveling bag she had.

"Oh sure, does it have wheels?"

"No, sorry."

"No problem, I'll carry it." The boy hoisted the case and she followed him. His dark skin was stark against the white shirt he wore, and his accent reminded Susan of many of the stewards and cooks who worked within the ship.

They took the elevator to the lower deck and did some more walking; in moments they were at the door of the Captain's quarters.

He knocked.

The captain answered. She expected to see something from *The Love Boat*, but instead, a heavy-set man sporting a cropped black beard looked down on her. His badge read, "Captain Starling." Well, the name almost fit.

"Susan," the captain said, extending his hand. "Come in."

Susan wasn't sure what she expected, but somehow she hadn't counted on the police. Officers Kealoha and Levine stood waiting. There wasn't time to look over the awards hung within the captain's quarters. She was being directed to a chair.

Captain Starling sat and the two officers followed suit.

"So, Susan," said an almost too-eager Levine. "We hear you were walking the ship very early this morning."

"Well, yeah, sure. I ah, took a little walk."

"What would you need to go down to the storage hold for?"

"I...well, Mrs. McLean was down there, too."

"She was expected. What about you?"

"I was just curious."

"About what?"

"You know."

"Tell us."

She felt like a child and the captain was shooting bullets with his eyes.

"That man, I just had to know he was alright."

Kealoha smirked. "He's dead, Ms. Cramer."

Her heart was beating like a band drum. How in heaven's name was she going to get out of this one? And then a new thought appeared. "Mrs. McLean, Sylvia, she needed me. I couldn't find her in her cabin and I searched everywhere until I found her."

"But Ms. Cramer, you didn't go in the direction of Mrs. McLean's cabin," the captain chimed in.

"And how would you know that?" Susan knew exactly how they'd known. They'd watched her through the cameras; they knew every step she'd made this morning just as they knew every step she was making now.

"Ms. Cramer. You have to understand something. This investigation is serious. A man has died on board. We have to know you weren't involved." Kealoha again.

"But I wasn't involved!"

Kealoha tapped his golden ring against the arm of the chair.

"Well, I wasn't, and I'll prove it!"

***

Leaving the ship, escorted by the police, was the hardest part. As she stepped away from the *Aloha*, Susan breathed in the humid air. Turning from the dock she eyed the ship one last time, hoping beyond hope one day she'd be able to take a cruise again.

When her phone rang out a catching Hawaiian tune a few hours later, Susan answered. "Hello," she said.

"Susan is that you?"

"Henry."

It was Monday afternoon, and the hotel the police had decided to shelter her in was of the cheap variety. Susan had almost laughed when the two cops had ushered her to the door of Hotel City in Kahului. It was like going back in time—almost.

"I've just got in. I'll be up to your room in a minute." It was her second day in Maui, the third day of the *Aloha* cruise (though she wasn't on it), and he was finally here.

Susan breathed a sigh of relief.

"I took the first flight out, and then took a jet to the island."

"How early is it?" Susan asked.

"Look at your clock."

19

The time was 3:34 p.m. "I guess I slept for awhile. The past two days have been terrible. I was behind lock and key the entire time answering questions."

"Probably needed it."

"The lock or the time?"

"Both." She could almost feel Henry smiling from the other end.

Susan thought of all the times she hadn't allowed Henry in, but life was different now. She said a quick good-bye, and gathered her pajamas around her. She'd probably just have enough time to change her clothes, but she couldn't wear these. And the *Aloha*? It had already departed without her.

Slipping into the bathroom she collected her shorts and a T-shirt. By the time she'd brushed through her brown hair, Henry was at the door.

"What's that musty smell?" he asked the moment he stepped in. She'd already made the bed. The cover was a sort of brown and beige monstrosity with a hint of puke green, and she'd cleaned off the particle board end table. Still, there was a television set (such as it was) and heavy enough drapes to cover up the less than fantastic view next door.

"Probably dead rats." She waved her arm in the direction of the bed. "You can put that there."

Henry held a gleaming black suitcase and his red hair was slicked back on either side and parted in the middle as always. He was wearing tan shorts and a blue shirt buttoned at the neck. It made his red hair look even redder. As always, he was as slim as a reed.

He turned, smiling at her. "So, you're involved in yet another mystery," he said, breathing wearily. "I'm glad you called me. Besides the fact I'm bored to no end with that desk job, I was missing you something fierce."

If Susan blushed she didn't know it, though Henry blushed enough for both of them. He placed the suitcase on the end of her bed and sat down, patting a space by him. She could feel the springs between the mattress as she sat, even with the comforter on, and wondered how she'd ever have a good night's sleep.

"I'm shocked. You must have a knack for murder."

Now it was Susan's turn to wonder. Perhaps she had a gift for detective work, or at the very worst, some sort of murder magnet attached to her skin.

"Why do you think I keep seeing these murders?" she asked.

"Heck if I know." He smiled over at her. "But I think we're a pretty good team."

She thought of all the bungling that had occurred during the *Scrambled* case and didn't agree. "I'm not sure I can do this again."

Henry patted her knee. Because it was exposed she could feel the warmth of his skin.

"Tell me all of the details," he said, "and I'll take you out to an early dinner."

***

It was with relief she and Henry had managed to escape the confining room and travel to a fairly local sit-down restaurant, the *Aqua Palms*, a "dive" just off the western shores of Maui. The place wasn't fancy, but neither was Henry James. She was just glad for a bit of a reprieve.

The place was packed, and it took a moment for the server to sit them.

"*Aloha!*" she said, her grass skirts swishing against the table. "Welcome to Aqua Palms. Would you like to try the loco moco today?"

Susan grunted. And then she snorted. And then, quite frankly, she was embarrassed.

But Henry was smiling. "Actually, Susan, I have heard the loco moco is a specialty around here."

The waitress nodded. Her long chestnut hair was pulled back into a tight pony tail, and her dark eyes blinked in appreciation. "The loco moco: white rice, a hamburger patty, one sunny-side up egg, and gravy."

"Wow. Sounds like a winner."

"I think you should try it," Henry said, his eyes on her. "Besides, it's the best food you can get here. The only way to get a real taste of paradise."

Susan surveyed the walls. Painted a burnt stucco orange, the framed photos, which graced the bright walls with their various

Maui scenes, eased the initial shock and appeared to breathe in new life. A sign above them displayed many a customer's future pleasure. "Your comfort is our #1 goal."

Susan wasn't sure how comfortable she'd be here, but she was plenty hungry.

***

The next morning the loco moco had digested and Susan was feeling like she was almost back to normal. The police had spoken to her an additional time and she'd given them the same answers because they'd asked her the same questions. That is, all except one.

There seemed to be some confusion on the wine Joe McLean had ingested, something the police figured wasn't poisoned after all. By the end of the interrogation, Susan was wiping her brow and Henry was pacing the room.

"I think I see what you mean," he said, parting the heavy drapes and looking out. "You're probably going to be hanging out here even longer than I thought."

"How long?"

"At least a few more days, so let's make the best of it."

Susan wondered what Henry meant. Their relationship was still platonic, and Susan hadn't planned on taking it any further. They hadn't even kissed. But Henry had held her hand and occasionally, like today, had made references to life as a couple she couldn't even begin to think about.

"So, what do you have in mind?" she asked, leaving the bed and taking a position next to him near the window. The man didn't stir. She could almost feel his heart beating, but she waited, curious of what he might say.

"I'll help you," he said, "solve this murder so we...you can go on with your life."

***

The next day she and Henry spent some time on Kaanapali beach in Maui gathering shells. She still had her colorful gathering bag and she would use it.

It was the perfect day for a walk, and Henry held her hand and they walked within the waves, their toes squishing between the fine sand. Well, it might have been much worse.

They, meaning the police, might have locked her up in jail. They might have continued to question her until she went mad. Or she might have relented when Henry had suggested a snorkeling adventure at Puu Kekaa, or *Black Rock*, as the non-locals called it.

As it was she was taking in the sultry breeze and white sands of Kaanapali beach, spending some well-needed time at Whaler's Village and sitting back and taking a load off. The free Hawaiian entertainment was something Susan wouldn't be able to shrug off, if ever, for months to come.

And Henry was happy.

That night she hardly minded going back to the old hotel and watching the sun set with Henry at her side. The orange glow penetrated her heart, filling the sky.

Advice

"We need to get back on the ship."

It was Wednesday, and according to Susan's calculations, the *Aloha* had just docked in Kona after spending Tuesday in Hilo. The *Aloha* wouldn't be back in Maui until Sunday, and, even then, she wasn't sure if they could even board the ship.

"And how do you propose we do that?" she asked.

Henry was standing at her door. "You'd better let me in," he said.

Fortunately, the police were no longer watching at the door; they'd moved on to the lobby. He stepped inside.

"We need to get on the ship. Do some more searching. Talk to some people."

"But Henry, the ship isn't even here!"

"I know." He grinned, touching her lightly on the shoulder. "Wouldn't you like to know more about what happened? We may not be able to vacation forever. Besides..." He looked down at his phone. "I've been talking to the police here. They want us back on the job."

"You're kidding."

Henry blushed. "No. They feel bad about ruining your cruise and want to make it up to you. Besides, you do want to learn more..."

"More, about what?"

"The police seem to think Mr. McLean was murdered."

"I thought you said they couldn't find any poison in the wine."

"Yes, but folks can murder using poison elsewhere. Let me put it this way..." He rummaged through his pockets and brought out some hundred dollar bills. "I've got this money burning a hole..."

It was a set-up and she knew it. Still, she couldn't help laughing.

"Can a person join a cruise when it's already begun? We'll have to get on board at Honolulu where the cruise starts."

"Right, but I think we have enough money to do just that."

"Do you think the police will let me back on board...?"

Henry reached back inside his shorts pocket. He pulled out two tickets and showed them to her.

"How...?"

"Like I said, they owe you one."

"But what about you? You're only..."

His fingers touched her lips. "Only?"

"Sorry, I just meant..."

"I may be a desk man now, but I used to be a real good cop."

She smiled, small tears filling her eyes. Why was she crying? And why now?

***

It was time to check in at the disembarkation port at Honolulu and the lines were as long as those she imagined would be at Disneyland. She had to imagine because she'd never been there either.

Susan could hear little through the talk and excitement. Henry stood near her, almost too close, as if breathing in the same air she did, did something for him. Maybe it did.

Susan had to admit she enjoyed Henry's company, and in fact, she felt her heart speeding up whenever he was around; the feel of his hand as he touched her on the arm or shoulder made her heart beat even faster. It wasn't like him to travel (even with his hands) anywhere she didn't want him to, and because of the barrier she'd created, their relationship had remained simple and undisturbed.

Henry smiled down at her and then handed over the tickets. A gentleman with a crew cut and a white shirt with a flag on the left sleeve handed back the tickets after checking their paperwork and passenger documentation. They were given their cabin assignment, their key and Seaside ID card and an information packet.

"Follow the pathway there." The man pointed left and Susan looked up the walkway edged by theater barriers, the kind with the golden posts and red, velvet separators, (except these were made of metal and linked chain) and followed Henry.

The captain met them at the entrance, as also the crew, or the crew who performed special duties where the new arrivals were concerned. Captain Starling was quiet, but his eyes penetrated her own. They showed their tickets once again, got their pictures taken, which were then printed onto their ID cards, were asked to leave any food or drinks there, and ushered onto the ship.

Finding their stateroom took less time than Susan's first experience. This time her cabin was closer to the infirmary on the lower deck and Susan wondered if Henry had made the change on purpose. And then she realized something else.

They were unloading, she in her stateroom and he on the other side, when she realized Henry had taken Sylvia McLean's old room, and he had given her the room opposite. It was crazy, but smart in the way detective work was all about.

Finishing her cleaning she knocked on his stateroom door.

Henry answered. "So, what do you think about your cabin?" he asked.

"It's nice. But you have the ocean view."

Henry blushed. "Sorry. I didn't want you to get tripped up."

"You mean you thought I might fall off the balcony?"

He continued blushing. "No, nothing like that. Come in."

"So, this is Sylvia's old room." She looked at the walls painted a basic cream. The blue bedspread, with its off-white undertones, made her think of the waves just outside the deck window.

"Wasn't sure if you'd remember."

Now it was her turn to blush. "I was just on this ship a week ago, remember?" She looked around. Henry's clothes were put away and his suitcase was tucked inside the small closet.

"Why *are* the bathroom's so tiny?" she asked, peering inside to see a small shower, a tiny sink and a standard toilet.

"Maybe they'd rather have you fall in *there* when the ship's moving."

She laughed. "Or maybe they can fit more people on the ship if the bathrooms are smaller than the closets."

"Could be."

"So, did you find anything? Any evidence, I mean?"

"I haven't had time to look." In a blink he was fingering a light blue towel, folded in a sea turtle shape. "Isn't it amazing?"

"I wonder how they do that."

"I have no idea." Susan fingered the towel but she couldn't make heads nor tails of it. "I guess it will just have to be a mystery," she added, but Henry had already opened the stateroom door and was stepping out.

"You have to see it out here," he said.

Susan stepped out. All she saw was a wall. They were still docked.

"You're funny."

"No, the deck. The deck chairs."

Susan looked down to see two identical metal chairs made with a blue carpet like cushion running down the center. "Chairs?"

"Look at this one!"

Sure enough, one of the chairs looked like it had been cleaned within the last few hours. Susan could see a darker blue amidst the lighter shade on the back area. She touched it. The cleaning job was still wet.

***

"Let's get some loco moco."

"What?"

They were sitting at one of the deck dining areas. Bulbous white lights towered above them, almost hovering, and Susan wondered if the Spanish omelet she was eating would be enough. Not just for her stomach but for the interest of Henry James.

"Didn't you like it? I mean the loco moco we had at *Aqua Palms*?"

"Hardly. It was too much."

Henry licked his lips. His omelet was already half eaten. He was actually thinking of eating more.

"How can you fit everything…"

Unlike her ex Husband, Henry was built like a reed and about as skinny as a tent pole. It was amazing what the man could put down without gaining in the middle.

She smiled over at him. "So what do you think the stain was in your stateroom?"

He shrugged. "Probably wine."

Henry stood up and carried his plate. "I'll be back in a minute," he said.

But it wasn't a minute, and after a half an hour, Susan went in search of him.

SUNNY SIDE-UP

Secrets

"What are you doing in here?"

Henry looked at her wide-eyed and continued searching under the bed. They were in his stateroom.

"Why didn't you come back? Did you eat the loco moco somewhere else?"

"Of course not. You wouldn't believe who's here."

"Who?" She watched as he peeked leisurely underneath the bed.

"Sylvia McLean!"

"Under the bed? She wouldn't fit! In fact, you're the only person who would!"

She heard his laughter as he continued to search.

"She left the ship after her husband's death, didn't she?" she asked.

"Couldn't have. She walked right passed us while we were eating..."

"But you've never even met the old bat…"

Henry smiled. "The police, the ones who interrogated you, they showed me a picture. The eyes, they're the same...But it wasn't just the eyes. The face, it was the same face, I'm pretty sure it was her."

Susan picked a piece of white lint from Henry's hair. "Well, it just doesn't make any sense. Sit down so we can talk about it."

"Funny, she was wearing a white uniform like she worked here or something."

"Worked here? Why would they hire an old woman in her eighties..."

He stopped and looked at her. "She was much younger."

"How old?"

"She looked around 20 or so."

"Then it couldn't be Mrs. McLean, could it?" she asked.

Henry blinked. It was as if he'd discovered his mistake for the first time. An old woman and a young woman inhabiting the same body?

"Look, there's no way this could be the same Mrs. McLean," she said, taking him by the hand. "No way. Let's take a walk."

***

After an unhurried dinner in her stateroom, they'd taken a trip to the breakfast area only to find a different set of workers cooking, cleaning and getting ready for the next tourist onslaught. The ship was on the move now and the water crashed against the ship and the sun was high.

That's when she saw Charles, the ship's medical officer, the man who had come to her aid after Sylvia's terrified scream. He was wearing the same white shirt and shorts and his white hair was cut short around his large ears. Would he remember her?

"Excuse me."

The man looked at her wide eyed. "Yes, ma'am."

"I was wondering about the woman working on deck this morning around 8 a.m."

"Name?"

"Rose," Henry offered.

"Rose Anderson?"

"Perhaps. Could we speak to her?"

Charles turned to face them. "It couldn't have been Rose. She isn't allowed on this part of the ship."

"Why not?" Henry asked.

"Well, she cleans the rooms. That's her duty, nothing else."

"Well, I'm pretty sure I saw her," Henry said. "I read her name tag."

Charles blinked. "Listen, I won't tell if you won't," he said, pointing in the direction of the cabins, and forcing a smile. "Rose is more than likely cleaning the rooms." He looked at his watch. "You should find her middle deck somewhere. But I'll warn you, she'll be in big trouble if she's caught talking to you."

Susan nodded. They turned in the direction the man had directed. It took them nearly half an hour to find her. The woman was picking up and disposing of some paper in the room; pushing it into a garbage bag on wheels.

When she looked up, Susan could see the resemblance of the old woman, but she was young, far to young to be Mrs. McLean.

"We just need to ask you a few questions," Henry stated when she looked up.

"About what?"

"Let's start with how long you've been working on the ship."

"This one in particular?" she offered, brushing a long, dark hair from her brown eyes and working her hair into an elastic pony tail.

"Yes, this one."

"Well, let's see… about 5 years I guess."

"And, are you married?"

Rose, a tall gal with lengthy legs, looked into Henry's eyes and smiled. "Why do you need to know?"

"Just wondering. My friend, Susan here is considering finding work on a cruise ship."

"But why ask me?"

"We were…just passing by…" Susan offered.

"Married?" Rose asked, looking at her.

"Ah…I was."

Rose smiled again, leaving the paper mess, and walked closer. Susan noticed her perfect skin and the way her dark eyes lit up as she looked at Henry.

"Oh, uh, when was the last time you were on the ship?"

"Last cruise." She turned to the door.

"Did you hear about the man who died on board?"

"Man? Actually there were three at last count."

"Three?" Susan asked.

"Let's see...there was a child, one man and one woman."

"That's a lot," said Susan.

"Deaths occur on cruise ships, though usually much less." She turned from them. "I think you'd better go. I'll be skinned alive if they find me talking to you." She paused and turned back, looking into Henry's eyes.

***

"So, why were you staring at her like that?"

"You know, her voice doesn't sound anything like an old woman's. I suppose she could have disguised it, but…it may just be a feeling, but I think I was wrong about her…looking so much like the old woman."

"That's only because you want to date her."

Henry stopped walking and placed his hand softly around her waist. "Why would I want that young woman when I already have a beautiful one at my side?"

"No really." She probably colored but she didn't care.

"You haven't a clue, have you?"

"And neither have you." Were they speaking about the murder or something else?

"Listen. No matter how you feel about me—right now—I'm determined never to leave you."

"Really?"

"Remember that day when you were boxing up the stuff to leave the *Hotel Camaro*?"

She nodded.

"Remember how I looked at you when you started packing that broken cup?"

"How?"

"Even when I knew you as Jenny, I could see there was something about you that was broken and needed to be fixed and…"

"You were determined to fix it."

"No."

"You didn't want to fix me? I thought all men wanted to fix the ones they loved."

"Oh, so you're saying, I love you?"

Susan's heart skipped a beat as she changed the subject. "Come on, what do you think the captain would say if he knew we were trying to solve a murder?"

"He already knows."

Susan remembered the look she'd received upon entering the ship in Honolulu, and figured the captain had a slew of information stored up in that brain of his he would probably never divulge. Still... if they never asked...

Captain's Quarters

Saturday night, following their departure from Honolulu, Susan and her companion had a few minutes to look at their surroundings before the questions began. It was near 9 p.m. and the captain, against his personal "wishes" had granted them a short meeting.

The awards on one wall contained photos of captains who had sailed with the *Aloha,* and to the right, a full living room, what looked like a separate bathroom with the door shut and a small kitchen. There was no balcony Susan could see, but the place was spacious and much more luxurious than she remembered.

"So, what do you want to know?" he asked. "I have many other duties to perform."

"The video. We'd like to view the video," Susan said.

"You mean the ship video? I hardly…"

"What Susan means to say, captain, is there may just be some evidence on tape we haven't yet considered."

Captain Starling smiled. "You are a part of what is being considered, and I find it odd you would want to incriminate Susan further."

"Not Susan, of course," said a bright-eyed Henry James. "Just the old woman."

"What old woman?"

"Mrs. McLean."

"She has disembarked," he said. "Watched her follow her husband out myself." There was a look of something hidden beneath the surface of the captain's words. He stood up and offered them the door. "It might be a better idea if you focused on Susan."

He smiled again, and Susan looked passed him. So many pictures, so many rooms...

"Yes, captain, but I also want to clear her name."

"Let the police do that, or the police on shore. They have the tape anyway."

"Why didn't you tell us that in the beginning?"

The captain ignored him.

"Have you seen it?" Henry asked.

"Of course. That's how we found...Susan here."

"Well, yes. What I meant was, what time was Mrs. McLean in the hold? What time did she leave her cabin?"

The captain shrugged.

"I thought you viewed the tapes."

The captain was angry. "Look. The woman went to see her husband at the medical officer's request. It's all on tape. Now, if you'll excuse me..." He opened the door and without another word ushered them out.

***

An hour later, Susan and Henry were in a turmoil of words.

"They what?"

"I'm quite serious. It seems Mr. McLean wasn't poisoned by the wine. The fish did it."

"The fish?"

"Somehow, Joe McLean got a hold of some bad fish."

Susan could hardly believe her ears. "So the wine for sure had nothing to do with it."

"Nope. The police are saying it was an accident."

"So we're done?"

"Naturally."

"What happens now?"

"Probably some court stuff with the cruise line."

"Do you think that's why so many have died?"

"Could be." He sighed. "Aren't you glad it's all over?"

They'd reached his cabin door. "How about we attend that disco dance they have going tomorrow night?"

"No."

"Oh, come on Susan, or should I call you Jenny..."

A chill as wide as Texas traveled up Susan's back but she said nothing. Henry was unlocking the door that led to the deck outside. "I want to enjoy this cruise, how about you?"

Susan looked out at the silver-blue ocean and listened. It was almost 10 p.m. and, as yet, they hadn't experienced much of anything fun since arriving on the ship. Still, there was something strange about dropping a case just because a man had died of accidental fish poisoning, especially since she'd never heard of someone actually dying from it.

"So what kind of fish did the man eat?" she asked.

"Tropical fish say the authorities, something called amberjack. Symptoms include diarrhea, numbness, rashes, anxiety, dizziness and more."

Susan sighed. "Some of that makes sense," she said. "McLean had rashes on his face, and what I thought was drunkenness, was probably dizziness from the poison. But something doesn't add up. I can see getting pretty sick after eating tainted fish, but the man died."

Henry took her by the waist. His arm felt warm, but the security she felt was fleeting.

"Evidently there's a point one percent chance of death from ciguatera poisoning," Henry returned.

***

"Good evening, Ms. Cramer." It was the steward, Jacob, coming up the hall and he was smiling, his large, white teeth filling up his face. "Do you have a few minutes?"

It was Sunday morning, and she and Henry had planned on taking a dip at the ship's pool. Susan's hand was propped, ready to knock on Henry's door.

The steward looked up and down the hallway. "In your cabin, if that's okay." He seemed to notice her hesitation. "You can keep the door propped open if you want to."

Susan turned back to her stateroom, propped the door open with a clothing iron retrieved from the bathroom wall, and invited the young man to sit on one of the cabin chairs. She sat in the other.

"I know what you're doing back here," he began, "and I'm glad you've come."

The room felt stuffy, almost musty. Was the smell coming from Jacob or had she forgotten to hang the wet towel from her shower to dry?

"I've been watching you."

"Have you been in my room?"

The boy hesitated, his large eyes growing larger. "Yes, but just to clean it."

"Are you sure?"

He hesitated again, and then ran his fingers through his dark hair. "I heard you earlier."

"When...earlier?"

"Now promise you won't get angry...or turn me in...until I've told you everything."

Susan's heart was pounding but she tried to remain calm. Her eyes scanned the door. The iron was still in place.

"I've heard all about you," he said, "about how you were there when the old man croaked, and how you've been trying to find the murderer..."

"But the man wasn't murdered."

"I guess you've heard that too," he said, "but it isn't true. I know it."

Susan pressed her hands in front of her. In that moment the small, round table in-between them felt like a well-needed space.

"How do you know?" she asked when the boy didn't continue.

"I heard them talking...the chief medical officer and the captain. They are worried about you being on the ship; something about you putting your nose in what is none of your business."

"And what business is that?"

"I wish I knew."

"What did they say exactly?"

"Charles, the chief medical officer, was supposed to watch you like a hawk and report to the captain if he saw anything strange. I have no idea how many more of the ship's crew have been asked to do the same."

"And you?"

"I...I was about to clean the captain's quarters when I realized how involved you wanted to be in the murder investigation.

I was there earlier today when you met with the captain." He stood, walking to the door.

"You were? I didn't see you."

"You can hear a lot with a cup on the door."

Susan stood. "So you think Joe McLean was murdered?"

"As sure as I'm standing here." He smiled, pushed open the door, and reaching down handed her the iron. "Oh, and one more thing. You need to be careful of Rose."

"Rose Anderson? Why?"

"She's been spying on you like no other."

Susan's heart resumed its quick speed.

"She doesn't look American to me. Is she?"

"Hardly."

"Is she married?"

"I have no idea."

She looked from Jacob's eyes to see Henry staring at her. He was standing in front of his own door, key in hand. "Ready to go?" he asked. Henry was wearing bright yellow trunks; his thin, hairy legs peeking out from below them.

Jacob said his good-byes. She watched him as he left them, his firm, tan legs taking a journey in the opposite direction.

"What did he want?" Henry asked.

She didn't say a word but took his hand. In moments they were walking down the narrow hallway to the pool.

***

"You want me to do what?"

Sunday had come and gone; even the dance had been somewhat surprising, but nothing to write home about. It was Monday morning, their second day on Maui. Because Henry had wanted to sleep in, she'd come up with her own plan. She'd wanted Jacob to search out Rose's room, but with a brush of his hand, Jacob had quickly stopped her.

Evidently all the fancy clothing was kept in her friend Candace's stateroom.

She was surprised, and he blushed. "Okay, so she's some sort of raptor.

41

A slight chill raced up Susan's back. "Raptor?" *What did being a raptor have to do with fancy clothing?* she thought.

"You know, like on Jurassic Park."

"I sort of guessed that."

"Rose isn't a woman who likes to hear the word no, and I have to work with her, so I try to string her along a little bit. She has her own place, of course, but most of the time we stay in my room."

"Does she dress up for you?"

The boy gulped. "Sometimes."

"Has she ever dressed up as an old woman?" She wasn't sure why she'd asked it, but there it was standing within her imagination in gray hair and wrinkly leotards.

The boy blinked. "Once. And it was pretty effective, I can assure you, but if she'd wanted to turn me on the result was quite the opposite."

Susan smiled. "I need you to take a photo with your phone. You do have a phone?"

The boy nodded.

"Maybe a wig, a dress, something like that."

***

The next day, Jacob returned with a photo of a wig. It was short and stunted like a shaved mouse with black streaks. Another photo revealed a gold dress.

***

By Thursday the *Aloha* had traveled to Kauai before Susan and Henry were able to put two and two together. The dress was exactly what Susan had seen on the woman. The hair? Well, it wasn't anything like Sylvia had worn on the night her husband had been murdered – that is, if Henry was right.

Two pieces to one puzzle, but neither one matched.

In total, the pictures on Jacob's cell consisted of a pair of nylons, three dresses, two broaches, a case of pancake make-up, fake fingernails and other old-lady paraphernalia that began to remind Susan of her previous friend, Ms. Martha Boaz from the *Scrambled* mystery.

She thanked Jacob, invited Henry to her stateroom, and sent the boy off.

"You should have had him photograph everything," he said. "And you should have told me what you were doing."

"How could I do that?"

"We're a team. It was a good idea for the most part. What if he'd been caught?"

"He could have just said he was looking for Rose...or something." She coughed. "You're right, I should have told you. So what do you think? The gold dress; it's the exact one.

"You've got a point. But not much evidence."

"What do you mean?"

"All we have is a dress and some accessories. What do you think about taking an excursion off ship today? Walking the seashore? Taking in some sights?"

As much as Susan was interested in learning the murderer's identity, they were in Kauai after all. It wouldn't be right not to journey outside for a bit.

***

The *Come and Get It* Souvenir Shop near Kalapaki Beach held every lava-lava and floral shirt imaginable, and there were picture frames, jewelry and other adornments Susan had never before considered as take-home gifts.

"I like this floral ring," she said to her companion, thinking of the dance now, the dance where he'd first held her in his arms. Although most of the songs played had been of the John Travolta type, all pointing and hand waving, this one had spoken to her in a lightning bolt. He was looking down as well, tinkering with the silver ring with pink, flowered stones as if he was eyeing an engagement ring.

"Now, try not to get any ideas. I just like it."

"I want to get it for you," he said.

"I'll get it for me," she said, and asked the clerk the price.

The price was manageable, a mere $15, so the item was paid for and placed on Susan's forefinger.

"So, what's next?" Susan asked, eager to continue. She was having a splendid time.

"How about the beach? Up for some shell searching?"

"Again?"

"It will give us some time to talk over the murder," he said, reaching for her hand.

They walked about 10 minutes to the pier and found themselves with a small crowd of folks lounging or playing near the water's edge. Though numbers were small, she also knew weekends drew a larger crowd. Again, Susan couldn't get over the fact the water was so blue.

She dipped her toes in the coolness, and breathed in the salty air. She was well beyond this world when Henry nudged her. "Look over there," he said, pointing in the pier's direction. "Doesn't she look familiar?"

Sure enough, Rose was at the foot of the lengthy bridge, dipping her own toes into the water and holding hands with someone.

"Looks like Jacob," he said.

Susan had to agree. "I didn't think he liked her. I mean, he seemed to be just messing with her head. What did he call her? Oh, yes, a raptor."

Henry was grinning. "I can see that."

"Why would Jacob warn us about staying away from Rose if it was his intent on getting close to her?"

Henry pushed his right sandal in the sand and a few grains leapt in front of his toes. "I wonder what's up."

"Me too. Do you think we should follow them?"

"I have a better idea."

The Search

With Jacob and Rose on shore, it was the perfect opportunity to go in search of their own evidence. But that meant getting back on board the transport boat and traveling to Nawiliwili where the ship was docked. Still, she was pretty sure they had enough time to look over Jacob's stateroom. But how, without easy access?

After a few fumbled attempts at trying to retrieve the key card themselves, they decided on making a visit to Candace's room, hoping she could shed some light on the subject. But they were in for a surprise. After explaining to her who they were, she seemed intrigued and walking to her purse, pulled out a blue card.

Holding a key card before her, she said, "Here, take it." She offered them no more information than where the room was located, and Susan wondered if the key had come with ease because the dark haired Candace had somehow discovered Jacob in her room as he was taking pictures and she wanted to get him back.

They were below deck, although they had been strictly forbidden down there, and already Susan was feeling a sense of doom. It was funny, but she was remembering her experience in the storage hold. It was darker in the hold too, and there weren't any windows.

The door opened and she followed her partner in.

But they were in for a surprise.

A young man with blond hair and a guitar in one hand leaned over a nearby doorway and inquired, "What are you doing here?"

Susan swallowed.

"Who are you?" Henry asked.

But the hippy seemed put off. "None of your business!" he hollered, making Susan jump. "Who are YOU?"

"This is a Glenna and I'm a... Frank."

The stateroom was a mess. A desk with a television set and clothing in multitudes was piled near him. The bed itself was a bunk bed, and Susan imagined Jacob sleeping on top. The blond haired boy sat in a folding chair near the entrance to the adjoining room. It was all she could do to stand there without her legs shaking.

"Ah...we're looking for Jacob," Henry said.

"Jacob's out. Think he went ashore. I probably should have done the same." He strummed a few keys on his guitar. The tune was ridged and a bit painful to the ears.

"Oh, well, we'll be going then."

"Sounds fine to me." He strummed again. "Next time, knock will you?"

Henry nodded, but the long haired blond was already enraptured with his next tune.

Outside the door, Henry touched her arm. "Sorry about that," he said. "We'd better get the card back to Candace."

"She should have told us Jacob had a roommate," Susan said, wondering again how they'd managed to get the key in the first place.

"There's something strange about this," said Henry. "Sometimes I wonder where my mind is. I should never have accepted the key from Candace without asking more questions."

"Like where she got it," Susan answered.

***

Vick Van Welton ran a close race with Red Skelton. He had a round face, bright red hair, and a voice that could soothe you one moment and flair your nostrils the next. The experience was like being on a roller-coaster.

Some sea sickness had set in since their journey and Susan was beginning to think she'd never get over it, and the comedian didn't help. Still, she was able to laugh as well as give an eagle eye to Rose when she walked across the stage as an old lady.

It was a surprise to see her, but then again, this particular puzzle piece was fitting together nicely. Why else would she dress up as an old woman if it wasn't to perform? Sure, she herself had been shocked at first, but now, watching her mannerisms like they were the dessert she'd recently had in the *Lemon Meringue Room*, Susan felt satisfied Rose was the best actor (at least of an old woman) she had ever seen. But something bothered her more than she could put a finger on.

After the show, she and Henry discussed it.

"Mrs. McLean had a different air about her. She wasn't funny or awkward, and much more emotional than Rose's part at the show."

They were standing on the deck where the murder had happened and Henry was searching for the wine spill. "They've cleaned up pretty well here," he finally said, ignoring her question.

"So what do you think?" The cool air breathed a seeming sigh against her cheeks, blowing her brown hair, making her feel like she was in heaven: almost. As she leaned into the railing she imagined the man again at her feet, a *sudden collapse* police were now calling an *accident*.

She shrugged. "All the other pieces fit. The dress, the girl dressing up."

"I know."

She felt an arm around her waist and didn't remove it. "Perhaps we're looking in the wrong place."

"I've tried contacting the police department here, but they won't tell me anything other than the case is moving forward. They're mainly concerned about you."

"They are?" This surprised Susan though she was grateful for their interest. She'd made some life-long friends at the police department back home, perhaps it would be the same here.

"What we need is an itinerary for Rose. What she was doing around the time of the murder. It would be great to see the video, but since..."

"We could ask Jacob."

***

"2 a.m.?"

"That's what I said."

Jacob squirmed a little. "Ah, she was with me. In my cabin."

"You're sure?"

The boy blushed. "Sure."

"What was she wearing?"

"Wearing?"

"Yes, wearing. You are trying to help us aren't you?"

Jacob stood. They were all in Henry's stateroom and the door to the ship's hallway as well as the balcony were shut.

"Maverick said you were acting kind of funny—nervous, as if you were trying to hide something," Jacob said.

"The man with the mane is Maverick?" Henry asked.

"If he has another name I don't know it. You might want to reconsider barging into a person's stateroom without asking."

"If we had to ask we wouldn't be barging," said Henry matter-of-factly.

"You don't trust me." The boy stood with his hands in his pockets and wouldn't sit. "Where did you get the key anyway? Maverick says you just let yourself in."

"Candace."

"Of course."

"So why would she have your key?" Susan asked.

He blushed. "We're old friends."

"What sort of old friends?" asked Henry.

"Friends, like I said."

"And we're just trying to figure out the truth."

"Behind my back?"

In an instant the room grew even smaller and Susan wondered why she had trusted the boy in the first place. It was obvious he liked Rose. But maybe he just wanted the truth like they did.

"Was Rose with you the entire night? I mean, when did you go to sleep?"

"None of your business. Anyway, I went to sleep late. Look, we'd had a few drinks and Rose and I were speaking about the gig…"

"What happened after that? Did you follow her to the show?" Henry asked.

"Oh, no, Rose gets nervous when I attend the shows. She asked me to stay behind."

"What time was that?"

"Well, the show starts around 8. I guess it was a few minutes before that."

"What did you do?" Henry asked.

"I watched a movie for awhile until I fell asleep."

"So you have no idea what Rose was doing at 2 a.m."

"She was asleep with me."

"Did you wake up at around that time?"

"No. But where else would Rose be at 2 a.m.?"

SUNNY SIDE-UP

Rose

Rose was talking to Charles on the *Raspberry Deck* when she and Henry spotted her.

"Do you have a minute?" Henry asked.

The girl smiled, her large smile filling her face, and then she saw Susan. "What do you need?" she asked.

"Some answers. Can we sit?"

Charles blinked his small brown eyes and left them.

"I'm still on shift. You'll have to talk while I walk around."

And so they followed her. The walk was a little dizzying, but Susan shrugged it off.

"You remember Joe McLean?" Henry asked.

"The man who croaked a few nights ago? Of course. When I heard it was a homicide I about gagged, but later, to hear it was merely an accident, relieved my mind a bit."

"Where were you about 10 p.m. on Saturday?"

"The night the guy croaked? Well, let me see…I was with Jacob and then I had my show, a performance you could say."

"As an old woman?" Susan's heart pounded. She wondered if Rose could see it beating underneath her T-shirt.

"Of course. I go in while the comic is doing his stuff, pretend I'm part of the act, (he's at the really funny part, talking about some old people in coffins) and I walk by as if I'm one of the old people who's returning to their coffin. I get a laugh every time."

"What time does the show end?"

"Around 10 on Saturday."

"What did you do after that?"

Rose looked wearily into Henry's eyes. "As if you'd like to know," she said.

"Jacob tells us you stayed with him."

"And he's right. I just snuggled up to his warm little body and went right to sleep."

"You're sure?"

"Well, I couldn't do much else. Jacob was already asleep."

***

"So tell me more about Candace's room," Henry asked.

"Why do you want to know?" They were both in swimming suits and taking a break by the pool. A few children splashed in front of them.

"Maybe we're missing something. If Rose murdered Mr. McLean then how did she do it? How did she poison him?"

"Well, it obviously wasn't in the wine. But we know the fish was bad. How would Rose know the fish had *expired* so to speak? How did she know there was only a slight chance the poison you mentioned could kill a man?"

"Consider how old Joe was. He may have just gotten a little sick, and then being on board ship had just made it worse. The man was also dehydrated. According to police reports, the man and his wife had taken an excursion together before boarding. That might have been just enough, adding the tainted fish, to kill McLean."

Susan considered what may have happened if the man had fallen overboard. "So the cruise line's at fault."

"Not exactly." Henry held her closer and she could smell the aftershave on his skin. "It takes roughly four to six hours for the poison to take effect and Mr. McLean died at about 10:00 p.m., right?"

Susan nodded.

"Let's see, the man and his wife boarded the ship at 5 p.m. If he'd eaten the tainted fish at 4 p.m., he would have died between 8 and 10 o'clock. If he'd managed to sneak a bite that evening on board, say 6 p.m., he would have passed between 10 and 12 p.m., so realistically, he could have been poisoned ashore or aboard ship."

"Wow," said Susan, her mind reeling. "What do the tapes show?"

"Nothing, according to the Honolulu Police, but there is some video with the couple entering their cabin at 5:15. Nothing until the dance at 8 p.m."

"What does the tape show then?"

"Just the two dancing, that's it."

Suddenly, Susan thought of Candace's place. It was funny how her stateroom came into her mind, but there it was. She had smelled something in that room, but what? "Candace's room smelled strange, but it was more like fingernail polish and underarm deodorant," she said, changing the conversation.

"Really?!"

Susan giggled. It lightened the heavy mood the poison had brought in. "The room smelled like it had been closed up for awhile—like Candace had been in there for a few days in her old T-shirt without taking any time to enjoy the scenery, or like perhaps she hadn't been there at all. It had almost a closed-up feeling. Other than that, let's see…there was a ladder, I guess to the top bunk, to the door's left, and on top of the bed I noticed a CD player; one of those old types you can hook small earphones into. There was a liquor bottle on a small table near a black folding chair and a bathroom with the door closed. I also noticed privacy curtains traveling across the bottom bunk where Candace slept."

Henry seemed impressed. "Good job. Perhaps it would be interesting to find out what was in that CD player."

"Probably just music."

"Could be. But the liquor is also interesting." Henry thumbed his fingers on his chin. I wonder if Rose is actually living in Jacob's room and if so, why he's not telling us the whole story. Candace seems to be in a sad state. What do you think she does for work?"

***

Candace was on the upper deck when they found her. It took almost an hour. In-between then they'd made eye contact with Jacob and had said a casual hello to Rose.

Candace was wearing a cotton shirt with a matching white skirt. She jumped when she saw them, and brushed her delicate hand through her dark hair.

"Oh, it's you," she said. "I'm not supposed to be up here. You won't tell, will you?"

Susan shrugged. "Why would we tell?"

"We have our own, quote, *leisurely spot* but I hate it. I like watching the traffic. She waved them over to two lounge chairs closer to the pool. "So, what do you need?"

"We need to be honest with you first. We're searching for the murderer of Joe McLean."

Candace grabbed a small towel from a nearby rack and wiped her forehead. "I wondered about that. Ever since Rose brought me on board she's done nothing but lie to me and avoid me. I thought we were friends and then found out she had a boyfriend on board and wouldn't have any use of me."

"Do you work as part of the entertainment?"

"Hardly. I work in the infirmary as a nurse. I came because Rose didn't want to be alone. Plus, it was a fairly good paying job and the cruise line liked me. As for Rose, she said she needed *moral support* whatever that's supposed to mean. She has spent an entire two minutes with me."

"So what does she do besides spend time with her boyfriend?"

"Work, of course, and do that cheap bit for that Vick Van Welton guy."

"We've seen that," Henry said. "Pretty funny."

"Pretty cheap if you ask me. She spends her days working and her nights sleeping over at Jacob's—but I probably should be keeping that a secret, though she stores much of her stuff as you've already discovered, with me."

"We already knew," Susan said.

"So what do you need from me?" she queried again, still sitting on the lounge chair's edge. "I mean, I hardly see the girl."

"What about a few nights back? Did you go to the dance?"

"The disco on Sunday?"

"No, the one on the previous cruise..."

"You mean the one where the guy died? Nope. But I heard he'd been poisoned by fish."

"Who told you?"

"Rose. One of the few conversations we have had."

"Did she say anything else?"

"She just thought it was weird, a guy dying because he ate some bad fish. I told her people got sick all of the time on cruise ships, didn't she know that, and sometimes they died—especially if they were old. And then she changed the subject."

"So where were you the night of the murder?"

"In my stateroom, such as it is. I was depressed. Being a nurse is one tough job, especially with people dying right and left. Can I say that? I just wanted to be left alone. The good news is today I'm feeling much better."

She smiled but the smile was unconvincing.

"Do you happen to know what music Rose listen's to?"

"Oh, mostly Broadway stuff."

"Anything else?"

"Well, let me think. I think some of her CDs are related to learning theatre. You know, learning how to speak a foreign language, having the correct syntax..."

***

Susan was sitting on the *Raspberry Deck* with Henry and he was having another loco moco. It was afternoon, and the warm and inviting breeze lifted her hair and caressed her naked arms. She was wearing a red tank-top and khaki shorts.

"You're going to get fat eating that stuff," she said.

He smiled, a bit of hamburger sticking out of his teeth.

"There's little you can eat for breakfast, lunch, or dinner and get away with it," he continued.

"Do you think we should turn Rose's name in to the police here?"

"What? You crazy?" he swallowed. "They'll just think we're nuts. Besides, I bet you want to ah…catch her in the act…"

"Funny, funny, the cruise is almost over and she hasn't so much as talked with another man other than Jacob."

"I know." He took another bite.

"Maybe Jacob has more to do with this scenario than we think. What about following him again?"

"Well, as a matter-of-fact, this morning, when I knocked on your door and you didn't answer, I went out and did some of my own detective work. Jacob made one interesting trip to the ship's hold."

"Why didn't you tell me?"

"I was hungry, and besides, I'm telling you now." He reached across the table for her hand. She'd had it recently manicured and was enjoying her new set of red nails.

She took it. His hand felt warm.

"Let's take another dip in the pool and I'll tell you about it."

"Tell me about it now. Why did Jacob go down into the hold?"

"All I know is, he came back up with a small package wrapped in silver tape."

"A small package?"

"Yep. And it smelled just like fish."

Jacob

"What are you talking about?"

"The fish you brought up from the hold this morning," Susan said. Henry opened his mouth in a wide O but she continued. "We think you know more about Joe McLean's death than you've told us."

"That old crud?"

Henry nudged Susan. "Maybe we should go," he said.

Rose had just finished her old woman rendition, and she and Henry had followed her out only to lose her up the hall.

"You guys are nuts. I told you, Rose is the culprit."

"How do you know?" Henry asked.

"Trust me, I know. I'd follow her if I were you."

"Why?"

"You guys must be new at the detective work. Did you know she's been seeing a new geezer?"

"Who?" Susan gaped.

"Go and find out. He's in stateroom 150."

She and Henry were both silent as they walked the narrow halls to stateroom 150, but Susan's thoughts were in a turmoil. What would they find when they got there? Would Rose, even now, be kissing the man she hoped to soon kill for his money? Would they be toasting to something? Her life, and his ultimate death?

The door was unlocked, and as Susan pushed it open, she saw nothing but darkness. A cruel chill raced up her back. "Should we go in there?" she whispered.

"You're silly," Henry answered. He brushed by her and into the depths of the stateroom. "Follow me," he whispered.

Susan tiptoed behind her friend and soon enough the light switch was on and they were both enveloped by light. And something else.

An old woman wearing the same gold dress and gray wig was asleep on the bed.

Susan's heart leapt beyond her chest and her hands felt drippy wet as Henry tugged on the gray wig. In moments it was off, revealing Rose for who she was. A young woman dressed in old-woman attire. Her old woman make-up was as thick as cement, the creases and valleys expertly drawn. But she was as still as...

"Henry...Henry..." she gasped, touching her heart as if it would start up again just by the motion.

"What?" Henry's face was as red as his hair, and Susan had never seen him so happy. "Look at the make-up, it's running off here...on her neck," Henry squealed. He was just like a kid, and Susan's whole body was ready for removal.

"Henry!"

"What?"

"Check her wrist. Just check her wrist!"

Henry reached down and fumbled for Rose's wrist.

It was like one of those slow motion movies for Susan, where everyone takes their time and it seems like forever when the next scene will play out. Susan's eyes surveyed the room; the closed drapes, what smelled like fish on the end table, the eerie way the woman was lying on the bed, without even a blanket for a covering.

And in that moment Henry stopped. It was with a white face that he turned to her now, almost fumbling the whispered words: "She's dead, Susan, Rose is dead."

***

It was Saturday morning and they'd once again docked in Honolulu. Keith Kealoha and Dorothy Levine hovered over them. Susan had taken one of the chairs and Henry had taken the other. They were in the captain's quarters once again and Captain Starling was angry.

The room was like its own morgue as Susan's mind swirled with new thoughts. What would happen now? Would she and Henry go to jail?

The captain was breathing like he'd been shot, the white shirt he was wearing taking on movement of its own. It seemed to breath in and out, in and out, like something living.

Susan looked up at the awards on the wall, taking in the faces of past captains and *Aloha* cruise awards until her eyes stumbled on a name: It read, "Captain Joe McLean." Her heart tumbled. Why hadn't she noticed the plaque before? More importantly, why hadn't Henry noticed?

"So, what do you think I should do with you?" the captain shouted. A slight redness remained in his cheeks as she turned. Kealoha had her in cuffs; ditto for Henry on the other chair. Both cops looked at her as if they'd just discovered a couple of dead dogs. But they were dead dogs, at least when it came to life now that Kealoha and Levine must have considered they'd murdered Rose.

And what about the captain? If he was involved in the plot like Jacob suggested, he would be no help to them. Still, she had to try. She opened her mouth to speak but Henry beat her to it.

"Check the tape. It will prove to you what we've been saying."

The captain smiled, but his eyes were still angry. "We've just docked at the Honolulu port, and I'm going to be sending you with the police."

"But the tape," Susan echoed.

"I'll check the tape, in fact, they can have it. I'm sure it will be all they need."

Kealoha adjusted his lei. The huge ring on his finger glittered as he reached for Susan and lifted her from the chair. She watched as Henry was taken as well. He didn't speak. Was he sorry he'd taken her on as junior detective? Was he sorry he'd even stepped foot in Maui?

Her wrists felt stiff as she was led out of the captain's cabin, past the infirmary and out the ship's doors. She was furious. To calm herself, Susan looked up at the morning sky. It was the last day of the cruise, and they'd made it through the trip—practically unscathed. They hadn't had an opportunity to question the chief medical officer nor sneak back into the ship's hold.

But they'd managed to discover from the captain that the room where Rose had been found dead harbored no old man (in fact, no one currently occupied that stateroom). And they'd discovered the truth about Mrs. Sylvia McLean. It was only a matter of time before they knew the details of the ship's medical officer and why Jacob had murdered Rose.

***

The Honolulu Police Department office was practically empty as they stepped inside on that morning, near 9 a.m. the seventh day of their cruise together. Susan looked up to see a second floor and, at the large room's base, a thick, gray staircase. A long desk met her eyes as well as roller chairs with officers sitting in them. Other desks, some filled, some empty, were organized throughout the room. An elevator to the second floor was closed, and there were pictures above it of what appeared to be the station in earlier days. The place smelled of newness and paint.

She and Henry were led toward the long table and to a desk just past the elevators. They were offered a chair and their cuffs, removed.

"Would you like a drink of water?" Levine asked.

Henry was still quiet, but this time took Susan's hand. It felt warm and reassuring. "We're fine," he said. "I guess you two have jurisdiction here as well as in Maui," he offered.

"Seems so," Levine suggested, saying nothing more. "So, you two, what did you discover on the *Aloha*? It was quite exciting watching your travails."

Henry grinned. "So glad you asked." He turned back to Susan.

Susan couldn't believe it. "Why am I always the last one to know anything?" she asked.

Henry smiled again, but she had already let go of his hand. "You're a creep, do you know that? I want nothing to do with you."

"What about helping me find out who the murderer is?" His fine breath was burning down her neck.

She sat down again on her chair and turned her eyes to the two police officers involved in the cover-up. "It was Jacob, plain and simple."

"Are you sure?" Henry asked.

Kealoha smiled. "Try not to be angry with him. You two are a great team. What would have happened if you knew we were all in on it?"

"You mean the captain, too?"

Levine laughed, pulled a chair up beside her, and leaned in. "NOT the captain. The police force. No one but the police force here and in Maui, and of course Henry, knew about what we were doing. WE didn't want you to get nervous."

"Nervous... about what?"

"Us watching you."

"Watching me? How?"

"Cameras."

"The ship's cameras?" Now she was sounding stupid but she had to ask.

"Other detectives were on the ship with you. They filmed quite a bit."

Susan wondered if they'd put cameras in her stateroom or how they'd followed her off ship when she and Henry had taken a well-needed excursion to Kauai, but her worries were quickly eased, though not put to rest.

"We only filmed the suspects," Levine said.

Susan's heart pounded. It was one thing to have cameras on board ship, quite another to have cops running all over the cruise ship seeing what they could get, wasn't it? And then she remembered the sneaky business she and Henry had manufactured to get information from Rose.

"So, I guess it isn't against the law."

Levine brushed something invisible from her gray suit. "Public places are fair game for the police."

Everyone else was silent. "I didn't think you'd care," Henry said, "once you knew the filming was to catch the murderer."

But Susan did care. It was like she had no privacy, and the police department had used her once again to get what they wanted. She took a heated walk to the soda machine. Slipping a few coins into the silver slot she waited briefly for the Coke to clunk to the bottom. Retrieving the can she walked the police station halls, taking in the guns the officers carried, the long rifles held by others, the way some police officers were dressed, some in partial, island attire,

61

others in full-officer regalia. And she couldn't be moved from her thoughts. She just couldn't be moved.

***

"I'm sorry, it won't happen again." Henry appeared worried. As he stood by her outside the police station, all Susan could think about was the next time. There wasn't going to be a next time— couldn't be a next time.

What was she doing, pretending she was a cop, anyway? Sure, people died at her feet but she didn't need to do anything about it. She could just go on with life like everyone else. So why didn't she?

She had been crying too, but didn't want Henry to know. It wasn't fair. She'd saved for a trip to the islands and had only gotten two ashore visits. Even on board, she'd been watched. Well, she'd have to see that tape to believe she'd had some privacy.

"You have a great way about you," Henry was saying now. "You were needed on this case to find out the truth about Rose, about Jacob. He felt more comfortable with you from the beginning. He was able to talk to you."

"So what?" Susan sniffed, realizing she'd probably given away her crying.

Henry placed his arm around her and led her to the back of the station. She thought of *Hawaii Five-O* and smiled, though only briefly.

"I'm not angry," she said, "just disappointed. I just want to be included in everything, that's all. You know, when I was with my husband, he was always trying to fix everything, and I always felt as if I was a third wheel. He wanted a baby, he wanted me to work, he wanted to eat what he wanted, and I was the delivery girl."

"Quite creative, too," Henry offered, holding her close. It was the first time she'd allowed this closeness, at least face to face without music humming. Laying her head against Henry's shoulder she began to sob. It was funny standing outside with half a dozen narrow palm trees blowing above them. Why was she crying? So, she hadn't been told about the secret cameras. So what? Perhaps she would have been more nervous if she'd known, feeling as if they'd catch her doing something stupid.

But then again, perhaps she wasn't being truthful with herself. Sure, she hadn't liked hearing about the cameras and secret cops, but she just couldn't help but assist the police discover Rose Anderson's true identity, either. Yes, even after all of this.

SUNNY SIDE-UP

Multiple Answers

"The ruse of Mrs. Sylvia McLean is a common one," said Levine. "She uses it often on cruise tours. Because she's also a part of the crew, it's a journey made in heaven—at least where she's concerned."

"But how does she do it all?"

"What do you mean?" Henry asked. "She's on the ship, after all."

"Yes, but consider this. She works in the day cleaning cabins, and at night she does her bit part during the comedy routine. What is her husband thinking during this time? Where does she tell him she's gone?" Susan said.

"Good questions." Henry winked at her. They were still at the station, though inside now, and Susan was ready for a break. Her light skirt felt tight against her legs and the back of her neck was sticky.

"Maybe the old men slept most of the day or something," Susan offered. "Maybe she drugged them."

"Could be," Kealoha replied, his golden ring gleaming. "What we know for sure is Rose seems to have died the same way as Joe McLean. Can we be sure of anything? McLean was tested, and though the test couldn't prove he'd eaten amberjack, the signs were there. We should know about Rose in the next few hours."

"Do you think Jacob killed Rose for the money she'd already squandered from Mr. McLean?" Susan asked, intent on getting her questions answered.

"Probably," answered Kealoha, twisting his golden ring on his finger. "But can we be sure he killed Mr. McLean?"

Susan shrugged.

"Evidence. Anyone, and I mean anyone could have forced Rose to eat that fish."

"What do the tapes show?"

"We haven't seen the tapes from this past cruise yet. But we should know the truth soon enough."

Susan shrugged. "What of the child who died on board? Children typically stay away from fish."

"But some must like it," said Kealoha. "Or she died of some other cause."

It sounded like a final statement from Kealoha, and Susan had to agree. Although Jacob was discovered carrying fish down the hall on the cruise ship, no one knew where the fish for Joe McLean had come from. And there had to be proof his dose of bad fish had also come from the *Aloha* to put the appropriate offenders behind bars.

***

Susan took a break outside the station. It was late Saturday afternoon and her partner, Henry, was on his way to pick up Jacob before the ship sailed once more at 7. She could just imagine how the event would transpire.

Jacob wouldn't like it. He would probably put up a fuss and try to explain his way out of the hole he'd dug himself in to. He would tell them it was Rose who was the *culprit*, or some such nonsense, and would say he had no idea the fish was *tainted*.

It was close to 5 p.m. when Henry drove up. Interestingly enough, the police here rarely used the typical *police car* to do their rounds, and this car was living proof. The car was a green Ford, a little worse for wear on the bumpers and grill. It was furnished with a blue light on the roof.

Kealoha looked upset.

"The boy has vanished from the cruise ship. According to the captain, he left early this morning. The camera caught him disembarking near 4 a.m. and no one has seen him since."

"And no one probably will again," said a disgruntled Susan. How could they be so stupid as to leave him there and take her and Henry?

"We had to get you out of there," Henry said as if reading her thoughts. "Things were heating up and we wanted you safe."

So it was her fault. "I think we should go in search of him," she said. "Now that we're no longer on board, we can find Jacob and bring him in for questioning. What about the captain and the chief medical officer? Have you questioned them?"

"Sure," shrugged Levine, though there was something in her answer that bothered Susan. Levine touched her gun again and looked out a station window. Various cars, their colors as distinct as their owners, were returning and Susan had a sneaking suspicion she and Henry would be sent out again.

***

Jacob Carlson. He'd been with the *Aloha* for 2 years and during that time his record had been impeccable. But just a few months prior to Mr. McLean's death, he'd been found hiding liqueur from the hold in his own cabin. Yes, the captain figured he was taking it home to his family on Maui in-between trips. How he'd managed to get it, the captain had no idea. The liqueur was locked up tight in the holding area, and only the ship bartender and wine steward had access. But he supposed anyone could get to it if they knew the right people.

According to his police record, now placed inside a hefty envelope where puzzle pieces continued to be gathered, the captain had let it go at first, seeing as the boy was supporting his mother and younger siblings—but he had begun taking fish and other supplies—and the captain had put his foot down. One more infraction and Jacob was off the ship.

Only Jacob had taken off…

***

"So why aren't we going to find Jacob?" They were in a borrowed police car, it was Sunday afternoon, and Henry was driving up *Richard Street* in Makaha. They turned into a drive-way.

A white dwelling stood before them. The place was little more than a shack. Overgrown palm trees hid most of the house and the place looked deserted.

67

Susan watched from the car as an old man opened the front door. He was wearing island attire, from shirt to skirt. Sandals graced his feet. He stood before them like a native, hands on hips.

"Get off my property," he said. His voice was brief and quick, kind of like a horse whip. She wasn't sure if she should get out of the car.

"We're looking for information on Joe McLean. Are you his brother?"

"Last time I checked," the man said, "though it's not your concern."

"We're sorry for..."

"Nothing," the man ended, brushing his filthy hands against his flowered skirt. "So, what do you want now? I've been asked all the questions I care to answer."

Susan blinked. No, she wouldn't get out. She'd just listen to the conversation from the opened car window.

"How was the funeral?"

"Fine. Expensive."

She watched as Henry looked over at the man's house.

"What are you gawking at? We pooled our resources. Have you caught his wife yet? She killed him, you know. Killed him as sure as I'm sit...standing here."

"Found a...someone who matches her description in a stateroom," Henry offered.

The man turned white. "You don't say? Well, good. Got what's coming to her. Whose stateroom?"

"That's police business," Henry said, wiping his forehead. Moments later, she and Henry had discovered Rose dressed as the old woman, but George didn't need to know that. It would only confuse the issue. The heat was penetrating and an open car window would only work for so long. Susan was hopeful Henry would be quick.

"I guess you knew your brother was once a cruise ship captain on the..."

"That creepy ship! I told him to get off it more than once. Funny things going on there if you ask me. He didn't do it though and wanted to wait for his retirement. Could have been alive today, the fool..."

"What did he tell you?"

"About the goings on of the ship? Well, we'd need more than a few minutes if you were to know everything."

"Well, what bothered you the most?"

The man looked Henry squarely in the eyes, and then they gravitated towards Susan's. "Who's the lucky woman?" he asked.

"My fiancé," Henry answered.

"A bit of a looker," the man said. "So, what do you want to know about my brother?"

In the end she'd gotten out of the car and the old man had fixed them both some lemonade. She'd drunk the strong stuff on the rickety front porch.

"Don't look like nothing much now," said the man who called himself George McLean, "but once upon a time, this place and the house sitting on it was a real beaut."

"So what did your brother tell you?" Henry asked.

"People going missing...people dying...weird stuff like jewels being distributed among crew members; stuff that would make your hair curl."

***

"He's nuts," Henry said as they drove away, "but perhaps there's some truth in what he said."

They'd spent about 3 hours at Joe's brother's house and Susan was amazed at what they'd learned—and from a man who was tired of talking to the cops. But Susan had to admit Henry had a way about him people liked. Sometimes, he was like the best friend next door.

"So I'm your fiancé?" she asked, trying to imagine what he'd say to her next.

Henry blushed. "Well, you're almost my fiancé," he muttered.

"What?"

"Sure, we haven't kissed yet, but..."

"You're sure getting daring in your old age!"

"Old age? Who's talking old? Did you see that old man's skin?"

Susan had. It looked like those railroad tracks close to the *Hotel Camaro* where she'd opened her doors to children. Though

Jane Dove, her new assistant, was watching the place until her return, the place was still rundown and old in areas she had no control over. Like the railroad tracks.

"I think I'd better call Jane," she said now, trying to change the subject. "How much longer do you think we'll need to be here before returning home?"

Henry looked at her briefly and shrugged his shoulders. "I have no idea," he said. "Maybe another week. Will Jane be okay with that?"

Susan nodded. She thought of her first two children now visiting on a daily basis. She'd first met brother and sister, Oscar and Brianne during the *Scrambled* mystery, and now they were regular visitors at the hotel. Susan fed them, and sometimes clothed them. They had a place of safety when they needed it, and donors were constantly offering more help when it came to providing for the unmet needs of the children in the area. At last count, more than a hundred children were using the services the hotel provided.

"I'll call her right now," Susan said, "and let her know I'll be extending my vacation. That's all she needs to know."

More Questions

Susan and Henry returned to headquarters and discovered Kealoha and Levine were still out tracking Jacob; it was 3 o'clock. The two had called in once or twice, only to tell the office, despite unfavorable odds, they were still continuing their wild goose chase.

Rose's mother was of little help. A stocky woman with bleached hair and a smile that appeared more painted on than real, met them at the fence of her tiny home.

"My girl is dead, and you want me to cry more?" She practically spit the words.

Henry stood back from the fence as she did; neither wanted the woman to strike out—or to get his/her face wet from the newly released spit. "We're here to gather facts," whispered Henry.

"Figures. So what do you want to know?" The woman sniveled behind her hand.

"What did she tell you of a Jacob Carlson?"

"You mean the boy she met on board ship?"

"Yes."

"I didn't like him. He was always in her way. She was going to become an actress."

"We'd heard about that," Henry said, looking away for a moment. There was a movement he couldn't place on the left side of the house. "She was doing some scene in a comedy act."

"Not only that. When the ship docked and she was given a bit of a vacation, she'd get busy writing a play or practicing on her singing voice."

Henry nodded. "Did she ever tell you where Jacob lived?"

The woman grew silent. She looked behind her and then forward again. "No. It wasn't like her to share details like that."

"But you knew what she did for a living."

"Besides that." The woman looked away. "I've got a lot to do," she said.

"We have a few more questions."

"I'm done answering." She turned from them and headed to the house.

"I think she's hiding Jacob in there," he said. "If we go back for a search warrant it might be too late."

"So, what do you suggest we do?"

"Watch the house."

They got in the car and drove to the next block. Henry parked the car and together they hid themselves behind a tall fence surrounding the back of the Anderson property. The air was getting hotter by the moment, and as Susan brushed her forehead and felt the sweat accumulate underneath her armpits, she hoped Jacob would come out – and soon.

***

It was almost dark before a lone figure left Rose's front door and proceeded up the walk. His pace was slow, though he looked around him like an alley cat. The boy turned the corner. In just moments he'd see the parked police car, such as it was, and Susan wondered how they'd be able to retrieve the boy before that.

But then in a blink Henry had vanished from her side; a whirr of red speed past her as he raced behind the boy, tackling him to the grass.

"What?!" the boy screeched as he tried to wriggle free.

Susan ran. By the time she arrived, Henry was placing cuffs on Jacob and lifting him from the ground.

"What?! Who?" The boy spit, realizing who had a hold of him. The spitting motion reminded Susan of Rose's mother. "You guys?"

Henry walked Jacob to the car and pushed him inside, shutting the door behind him. Susan was about to congratulate him on his success, but Henry appeared winded. He was breathing funny, as if the air had been knocked right out of him.

"Can you drive?" he asked.

"What's wrong?"

"Drive...please."

The moist grass and a thousand other smells on Jacob's person permeated the car as she drove. Henry sat next to her taking in shallow breaths. Jacob was a silent icon of death in the back seat.

Finally, Jacob said defiantly, "If you think I killed that old man and my girlfriend, you're crazy."

Susan watched the road but she could feel Jacob's eyes burning into her back. She was suddenly afraid. Would Jacob notice the Henry's condition? Would he try to escape?

"Well?"

"Well, what?" Henry moaned.

"Do you think I killed them?"

Susan continued to drive. She looked over at Henry. His skin was a deathly white and his eyes were closed.

"I should have figured it out," Jacob said, shifting on the back seat and leaning closer to her. "When I turned that corner and saw what appeared to be a light on the top of your police car...What did Rose's mother tell you?"

Susan continued her silence, hoping what she was doing was right. But she had a sneaking suspicion she was infuriating the boy further. Her skin prickled and her thoughts continued to be on Henry. By the time they reached the police station Henry wasn't moving. He sat slumped on the front seat like an old rag.

***

"You should have never been running like that." Susan was crying and Henry was lying in a hospital bed hooked up to an IV. They'd already checked his heart. A heart attack.

"Now I know why you were given that desk job."

Henry smirked up at her. "I'll let you do the running from now on," he said.

"We should have been more careful. I knew you had heart problems, but I never thought..."

Henry's face was still pale, even after a night's sleep, and it seemed to Susan all the man's blood had been drained out of him.

Jacob was safely behind bars at the Honolulu Police Station, but all she could think about was Henry. How could she have forgotten?

"You know me," Henry wheezed, reaching for Susan's hand. "Do you think I can sit behind a desk for eternity?"

"Then we'd better get you a new job."

"Or keep people from dropping dead around you," he offered.

Susan tried to smile, he was making a joke after all, but the movement was difficult. They were alone in the room at the Straub Hospital in Honolulu and Susan was glad. For a moment at least they could talk without a stranger overhearing them.

"So, what do you do now?" she asked.

"Looks like I'm going to be laid up for awhile."

"Looks like it." A light sheet with blue and green dots was drawn over Henry's body, and though his head and arms were free, the whole scene reminded Susan of a mummy movie.

"Do you think Jacob's the killer?" she asked, hoping it wouldn't cause a problem for Henry.

"Maybe. Perhaps Rose killed the old man and Jacob killed Rose because he'd discovered a bit of information he couldn't live without."

"Could be. But what if the killer is the ship's medical officer or even, the captain? Remember the captain knew Joe McLean. His picture was hanging up in the captain's quarters."

Henry reached for her. She took his hand and they were quiet for a moment. "Can we just forget about the case for a second?" he said. "I have something to ask you."

But Susan's heart was racing; she wondered why Henry would interrupt her thoughts when they were finally getting somewhere. Still, his voice was halted, but speaking, and the words appeared sincere.

"I think...we should get...married," he said, his face blushing to a ripe red, matching his hair.

***

Susan sat at the old hotel and watched as a hand-sized cockroach scurried across the floor. Then she dialed Jane at the *Hotel Camaro*.

"Is that really you?" Jane asked. Her voice sounded just as Susan remembered it. Sort of like a lollypop with freeze dried onions on the outside. Jane was all about fun unless the situation had to do with children in neglectful or abusive situations. If there was a bad omen from a set of parents, she would know it, and the child would forever have a place within Susan's establishment.

"It's me. How are Brianne and Oscar?"

"Coming in steadily, especially since their mom's been sick."

"That's nothing new."

"This part should strangle you a bit. I met their father today."

"I thought he was dead." Susan was lying on her uncomfortable mattress. She sat up, taking in a few large flies that were finding their way to the window sill.

"Me too, but the man's taking care of the children now, while the wife's in drug rehab."

She was well aware of the woman's problems, but the thought that her husband had finally been found, caused a weary and frightening feeling to travel up Susan's spine.

"So, what's the father like?"

"Seems strong. I think he plays sports. Yesterday he was wearing this ripped sort of shirt, and you know."

Jane always said, *you know*, when she didn't want to say it and Susan loved this strange quality. Jane was about as brash, about as colorful with her language as a snail. But she could still make you think about your life or your children's lives. Like now.

"They've been by a bit less than usual, but their faces seem a little more cheery, if that's possible."

Susan loved Brianne and Oscar like her own, though she'd never admitted the same to anyone. Both children lived across the street from the *Hotel Camaro*, and had been a part of solving the *Scrambled* crime. With the children's accumulated good experience away from home had come other children and more donations. Susan had expanded her services to free food, clothing, and entertainment. She'd built a play area behind the hotel and had added a small game room on the first floor, which would soon have to be expanded. And that meant wall removal.

"Are you handling everything okay?" she asked.

"As well as can be expected," came the reply. "So when are you coming home?"

"Soon."

"That doesn't tell me anything."

"I know and I'm sorry. Expect a little more money in your next paycheck." She could envision her friend grinning on the other end of the phone. "I'm serious. It may be a few more days before they allow me to leave here."

"They still think you did it?" Jane asked.

Now it was Susan's turn to smile. "They seemed to, at first. But now I'm free and clear." She thought of the crummy hotel room she was still staying in and thought about making a huge change. Still, though she was paying for the place now, the rent was cheap.

"That's good. How's Henry?"

"Henry's okay, I mean, that's why I called."

"To tell me about Henry?"

"He's asked me to marry him."

There was a long pause. Susan wasn't sure what to say next and she hoped Jane would re-begin the conversation. She wasn't disappointed.

"You mean he finally did it?"

"You say it as if he's been thinking…"

"Come on, Susan, after you divorced your husband it's been all he's talked about. Other than your cooking. The day you called him, he came right over here and told me all about it, before running out the door. He said, *I've just got to ask her. Sure, we'll be tackling a murder investigation, but we will be traveling the islands. How much more romantic can it get?*"

"Lots, in my opinion," offered a disgruntled Susan. "He hasn't even kissed me."

"No surprise there. Maybe the opportune time hasn't come yet. Maybe he doesn't think you want to kiss him."

"He's in the hospital."

"What?"

"In the hospital. He had a heart attack. And now I have to say *yes* to his proposal so he doesn't have another one."

Hopeful

It was the next day Susan realized the real quandary. If she said yes, he might have a heart attack, so either way she was hung out on a line. What should she do?

She decided to avoid the situation completely and visit the holding cell first.

Jacob's lean arm reached through the bars. The cell was small, little bigger than a closet, and the items inside, including a rough looking bed and a dirty looking toilet were bolted to the floor.

She hadn't meant to sit so close, but getting her mind off Henry was the best answer to her misery. Jacob's arms were hanging through the metal, and though they couldn't touch her she realized he wanted to speak. She looked into his eyes.

"So, how long are you going to keep me in here?" he asked.

"No more than 36 hours. After that..."

"But it's been longer than that already! And besides, I'm innocent!"

His words whirled through the bar doors like a heavy wind. Was the boy serious? She'd finally been able to watch the ship's tape. Rose had appeared suspicious when she'd gone down to the hull dressed as the old woman, and earlier, as she'd gone off to play her part at the comedy act. There was a boat load against her, but now that she was dead, it was natural they take a look at Jacob. Besides, hadn't the tape revealed his entrance into Rose's quarters just an hour before she was pronounced dead? Hadn't the boy admitted he was in it for the money?

"Susan..."

Susan watched Jacob's eyes. Something was gathering. Was he crying?

"Look. I wanted Rose's money, but I'd begun to care for her, you know? It started out as a lie, yes, but through the months I'd decided I could take her money but I could never hurt her."

"You mean by taking her money?"

"No, by killing her."

Susan stood from the bench opposite the bars. She walked to the boy she'd known as a steward on the *Aloha*, and planted her feet a few inches from him. "So who did it?"

He motioned for her to lean in closer. "You can help me. They look on you as some sort of...joke...so they'll never guess you're working for me."

"A joke, huh?" Heat like flaming fire burned up Susan's neck. She hardly had time to reflect on his other comment.

"Sorry. I mean..." He motioned for her again and Susan stepped closer. The back of her neck prickled with concern but she ignored it. "I will give you everything you need to find the killer," he whispered, wrapping his arm around her shoulders and pulling her closer. The chills continued.

The guard standing by the outer door muttered something under his breath and walked closer. "What are you doing?" he grunted.

Jacob smiled. He let go of Susan's shoulder. "Nothing, officer."

The officer's eyes were on Susan. "Did he hurt you?" he asked.

"No."

"I'd advise you to keep a safe distance."

Susan nodded, stepped away from the bars and sat down on the bench. The officer seemed satisfied and returned to his post. But in moments Susan could hear Jacob whispering something...

***

"We're alone."

Susan had hidden in the lady's restroom stall for over an hour before the place had closed up shop. Most of the officers were gone, though a few trickled in rooms where they'd sleep for the night.

78

The boy moved closer to the bars. "Look, you might think Rose killed Mr. McLean, but I have my suspicions."

"What suspicions?"

The room was dark, and the guard was no longer at his post. No one knew she was here, especially Henry who was still in the hospital. Thoughts of what Jacob could do as she sat next to him near the bars made her skin crawl but thoughts of gleaning some information trumped what might happen to her. The stuff of life that made her afraid trumped what she could learn if she just worked her way through it.

It had been the same way with her divorce. She'd expected her husband to just let her go, but the process had been angry and wearisome. He wanted her back; thought she was foolish to let him go; thought they could make it work. He was trying so hard, she knew that, but she also knew she no longer loved him, that it was all she could do to stand in the same room with him without feeling his love and her lack in return. Or was it pity?

She'd worked through the divorce and now felt freer than she had in years. Even now, as she sat slumped next to the bars, a possible killer on the other side, she felt as if she could do this. Perhaps Jacob wasn't the killer and he could give her valuable information, and she could solve this crime without Henry. She could prove to them all she wasn't, what had the boy said? A joke?

"Rose was one strange girl, but she was nice. Killing a man just wasn't in her nature. Sure, she dressed up as an old woman, and I thought it was pretty ingenious, but why kill an old man just for money?"

Susan smiled. "That's what the officer's think *you* did."

"But it just doesn't make sense. She'd just married the guy. He was an old coot, sure, but expanding the misery for awhile could get her more money. They were on their honeymoon, just starting out their life together."

"That's all Rose needed," Susan said. "She just needed to marry the guy to get his money."

"Yes, but how much money? Wouldn't she have gotten more if she'd been married to the guy for more than just a few days? And wouldn't the courts look at her with wide eyes; wonder about his sudden death?"

"Old people die on cruise ships all of the time. Besides, Mr. McLean was poisoned, though some are saying the poisoning might have been accidental. In my mind, either the man was poisoned before he arrived on board or he was poisoned while on board ship. The fish next to Rose is a good indication of how McLean must have died. Still, can fish really kill a person?"

"I guess if you're old enough," said Jacob. "But what if Mr. McLean's death was accidental, or at least made to appear accidental, what would the murderer hope to gain from that?"

A curious shudder ran through Susan's body.

"Money arrives fast in those situations," Jacob said.

"How would you know?"

There was some hesitation. "My father used to be a lawyer."

"Used to be?"

"He's dead."

"Sorry."

"Don't be, I'm not."

There was a sudden stillness on the other side of the bars and Susan wondered what she could possibly say next to smooth over the new feeling penetrating her heart. This boy had lost his father and probably had anger in his heart to match. And it didn't sound like they'd made up before his father's passing.

"I'm sorry," she said again.

The boy was silent. "You need to know even though he wasn't a good dad he taught me a lot about law. I know some stuff that would make your hair curl."

"Do the police know, I mean, about your dad?"

"They should, but I think it's funny they haven't asked me anything about him. Maybe it's because he's already dead."

"How did he die?"

"The drinking got him. He told me to never do it myself, but I had a hard time believing him."

Susan touched his shoulder and leaned in for the first time. She thought of the woman across the street, the woman whose children, Brianne and Oscar, were probably as far from her own thoughts as getting clean.

"So what do you know about the deaths? Do you think they were accidental?" she asked, sure the boy would relay what he'd already told her.

80

Instead he said, "If it can be proved Rose's death was accidental, it would be smooth sailing for the other party."

"What other party?"

"Her family, perhaps. Maybe they knew what she'd been doing to get rich and they wanted a piece of it."

Susan couldn't believe it. So someone, besides Jacob, wanted the girl dead to tap into her wealth. Well, one thing was for sure, it couldn't be her family. Susan couldn't believe a family would kill just to get money, but then, anything was possible if you were desperate...

"And then there's the other scenario," Jacob began, stepping back from the bars and looking away from her.

"What scenario?" Susan asked.

"Rose might still be alive."

The thought had never occurred to Susan. But hadn't she seen her dead with her own eyes? Still, she knew a body could appear dead without being dead, she had Henry to consider in that case; a pulse might be missed even by touch. These new thoughts made Susan's heart pound, and something else, something unmistakable.

***

"Henry, listen!"

Henry's eyes were open and he was staring at her like some strange fiend. It was Wednesday, just three days after his heart-attack, and he was still at the hospital, looking half drugged.

"Seriously? Rose still alive! Who put such a stupid idea into your head?"

Susan tried to weave her thoughts around the word, *stupid*, and instead told Henry all about the murder plan, except this time, she didn't tell Henry that Jacob had discussed the plan with her. She didn't tell him he was feeding her with information and that Jacob's father had once been a lawyer.

"It makes sense that all this time Rose was plotting to take Joe McLean's money. But alive? How can she be alive when we found her dead?"

"But *was* she dead?"

"Of course. I felt her pulse…"

"After that. Did you see her in the ship's morgue?"

"Why would I want to do that?"

"To make sure the death is an actuality."

"I suppose. But Susan, I saw a gurney being loaded from the ship, and all the records from the chief medical officer appear correct, and you heard Rose's mom. She's one angry camper about Rose's death."

"But what if Rose's mom is in on it?"

"You've been watching too many movies." Henry patted the left side of the bed. "Come and sit down. I want to hear about you. How have you been doing? Have you thought about the question I asked you?"

Why did he have to bring that up? Her stomach churned, and Susan was sure the churning wasn't because of what she'd just told Henry about Rose Anderson. If the girl, Rose, was alive, where was she hiding? Could the mother, Sarah, be hiding her along with the boy they now had in custody? And what of George, the brother of Joe? He must know something, since both his brother and his new wife were both dead. He must be getting a share of his brother's money. And what about the jewels he'd mentioned on their first meeting? Perhaps there was some truth to the statement after all.

"Well?"

"Well, what?"

"The question. What's your answer?"

"No, the answer is no." Susan couldn't look at him. She couldn't do anything.

George

When Susan left the hospital, she got into her rental car and drove to George's house. It wouldn't have been good to drive in a police car no matter how much it looked like a regular one; besides, it was against the rules on any normal basis and Susan didn't want people to know who she was from the outside anyway.

She stopped in the driveway and walked up to the door. The porch creaked and she watched a brown sliver of paint drift to the warped boards as she reached for the doorbell.

"Oh, it's you," the man said and opened the door for her to enter. "Where's your partner?"

She entered the room. It was sparse and made up of old furniture, old pictures, and old memorabilia; in one corner was stacked a newspaper pile almost reaching the ceiling. He nodded to a cover-torn chair. "You can sit here," he said.

Susan sat. She continued to survey the room, including the smell. It was worse than the *Hotel Camaro* utility room basement. The place reeked of spoiled rags, dirt and a thousand other smells Susan couldn't place.

She looked at him. George appeared to be wearing the same overalls he'd been wearing days before. He sat in the chair—such as it was—opposite, and strummed the arms with his thick fingers. "So, what will you be wanting today?" he asked. "Some lemonade?"

"I need to ask you a few more questions."

"About what?"

"Your brother and...and his wife."

"Shoot." The man sat stiff in the chair and Susan searched for guns on the wall, heavy objects the man might easily grab if the occasion arose. Unfortunately, the nearest item next to her was an old umbrella with a carved handle leaning against the chair. Still, some damage could be done.

She averted her eyes from the object and back to the old man. The creases in his face were lined with dirt and his fingernails matched the ensemble. He watched her without a smile.

"Your brother. You said he told you something about jewels. What kind of jewels?"

"Diamonds, rubies, that sort of stuff."

"What's the story behind them?"

"Well, someone's making some cash to be sure, carting it back and forth from cruise ship to shore and back again." He stared at Susan and she grew uncomfortable. "You knew he was a previous captain then of the *Aloha*. Good-bye, hello, it was all the same to them."

"Who is *them*?"

"The crew. Those who said my brother was getting too old to sail, to cart people around in the water." He touched his lips and remained in the same position, thinking. When his fingers were removed there was a distinct brown mark above his upper lip.

"I never told the cops this but my brother did have some previous psychiatric problems. They found out anyway, and used it to their advantage. But my brother was level headed, especially towards the end when he started to find out the secrets the *Aloha* held. Problem is, after he was killed they thought I was just as rickety as he was. They called me an *old man* right to my face. I decided to ignore it."

"Good idea." Susan smiled, thinking of the words that had recently come her way, words she wished she could forget. "So, how do you know your brother was killed? They say it was an accident."

"Like I told you the last time, they'll think of all sorts of reasons to keep themselves free from the goings-on within that ship. His wife was a real winner." He coughed into his dirty sleeve. "I told Joe it wasn't right to get hitched but he said he *liked her*, as if that was a decent reason to marry a wife. She was never good enough for him. Came around here about a month before they said they were going on a cruise. Wore a nasty gold dress the last time they came to visit. Wanted to know if I liked it."

"I saw her wearing the same dress on the cruise ship," Susan said, her mind going back to the night McLean was found dead on deck. She thought about Rose wearing it for the comedy routine, and in her mind's eye, remembered the glittering dress the night they'd found her dead.

"She said it was her special dress, as if somehow it held some meaning. Women," he added hastily, wiping above his lip. "I miss my brother, but not his wife. There just wasn't something right about her."

"What do you think that something was?"

"I'm still trying to figure that one out. She was fake. I know now she was young and all that, but she presented herself pretty old to me. I would never have believed she was young if the police hadn't told me."

"What about your brother's money?"

"What money?" George asked. This time he refrained from wiping above his lip and instead looked past her to the front door. "My brother didn't have any money."

"But what about his expensive funeral? Didn't you get anything?"

"As you can see by looking around you, I didn't get much." George stood and walked to the kitchen. On his return he held a golden ring with a large diamond in the center. "Joe and I always talked about me getting this ring if he passed first. If I passed first he would get my house—such as it is. Everything else went to his new wife's family."

"His wife's family? You're his brother!"

"Unfortunately, I'm the last living relative of any mention." He paused. "His new wife, however, has a gaggle of family members with wide open hands and plenty of need for it."

Susan felt terrible. Perhaps the brother could sell the ring and fix up the old place.

"I know what you're thinking," George said, touching the space above his lip. But I have tried everything. His will, the one that was filled out just before he went on that cruise was changed. All I have is this ring. And no, I didn't pay for his funeral or his wedding. His wife, she did that."

"When was your brother married?"

85

"A day before they hopped on board. I wasn't invited. You're looking at me strange as if you think it just couldn't happen. But my brother was a different man the day before he stepped on board the *Aloha*, a very different man."

***

It wasn't easy to return to the hospital, but by Saturday, and with no word from Henry, Susan ventured in. The bed Henry had slept in was empty. Checking with a nurse she discovered Henry's slip. He'd left the hospital when the staff was minimal and the place, silent.

They'd come to check on him near 1 a.m. only to discover an empty bed and a half empty water glass on the nightstand. There was no note and his clothes were no longer in the closet.

Susan felt sick. Henry wasn't well enough to leave the room on his own. Or was he? His clothes were gone, so obviously he'd put them on. Who had come for him? Was Jacob somehow involved, or George, Joe's brother? She raced to the police station only to discover Kealoha and Levine in a fight of words.

It was 8 a.m. "You're kidding!" Kealoha was screaming into the air. "No one saw him leave his room?"

"The reports…"

"Who cares about the reports?" Kealoha hissed. His island attire was anything but colorful now and the breath of anger filling his face made Susan flinch.

"So what are you going to do about it?" she asked. "He's gone, and why are you guys still talking about it?"

Kealoha jumped. "Oh, it's you," he said. "The sneaky one…We've been up all night!" He dragged a chair over for her and placed it next to Levine. "Sit."

Susan sat, but she couldn't remain still. Every inch of her struggled to understand. Who had taken Henry, and why? And what would they do now?

"I've spoken to Jacob. He appears to know nothing about Henry's kidnapping, but I have a feeling he wouldn't tell us the truth anyway, even if he knew it," Levine said.

"How can you be so sure he was kidnapped?" Susan asked. She grasped the chair's sides, her knuckles turning white. "What do you know about him anyway?"

Four curious eyes peered over at her. "And what, pray, do you know about Jacob Carlson?" Levine asked, her green eyes surveying Susan's like the ticking of a clock.

"Nothing...nothing."

"You know something. We saw you with Jacob. You do know there are cameras in there."

"Oh," Susan croaked. "I'm not sure," she added.

"Not sure? For a woman who wants to find her lover's kidnappers, you sure have a funny way of helping out." Kealoha again.

"I...I'm not his...lover!"

Kealoha smiled. "Well, you sure have a funny way of loving him then," he spat.

Susan's nerves were at their peak. She didn't like what police officer Kealoha was inferring, but neither did she like the fact that they were still yelling at each other and solving nothing. She gave a forced laugh. "You guys...you care about one thing, putting people into peg holes and leaving them there."

"What's that supposed to mean?" Levine was angry. She stood, and began to pace the room. "For your information, we're the practiced cops here. You come in here, and just because you're with Henry you think you know it all. I've heard about you, how..."

"Shut up, Levine!" Kealoha stood, facing his opponent. "We need to find Henry. There's not any time for this." He looked over at her. Susan could tell he was trying to smile, but his eyes were angry and his tense muscles did little to calm Susan's beating heart. She would find Henry, even if she had to look for him herself.

***

Jacob was quiet. They sat together in the interrogation room, she, Jacob and Levine. Kealoha had stepped out, hoping the women could get the boy to speak as he'd done before with just Susan in front of him.

But Jacob wasn't speaking now.

"We need to hear more about Rose," Susan was asking. Levine's lips were tight but she held her peace. In the corner she noticed the camera. "We need to know everything."

"I've told you everything. And I didn't mean for Susan to tell...you."

But Levine appeared nonplussed. "We need your help." She leaned forward, her suit coat tails sweeping the top of the sturdy table. Paper in hand, she asked, "You told Susan your father was a lawyer, and that he'd helped you in math."

"That's correct." The boy smiled, but it was more of a, *I guess I know even more than you* kind of smile and it appeared to prick at Levine's back. She sat up straighter and placed the paper on the table.

"Police officer Levine wants to know why you think Rose is still alive."

"She told me so."

"What do you mean she told you so?" Levine again.

"She was supposed to be dead. I thought she was dead like the rest of you." He paused and looked around. Susan wondered why. Besides the three of them there was no one. But there was that two-way mirror; a way for the other officers to look in from the other side. Maybe Jacob was doubting himself now or fearing something.

"But she isn't dead. Is that what you're saying?" Susan asked. "Did she talk to you?"

Levine gave her a quick look. Susan pretended not to notice. "Jacob, you can tell me. We're friends, right? If she talked to you after she was dead, she's got to be alive, right?"

"As sure as I'm sitting here."

"Where, I mean, when did she contact you?"

"Just after the gurney left the ship. It was eerie I can tell you."

"So she called you?"

"I had just left the ship, for a little r-n-r, I was freaked out because of her death and needed some space. I left the ship, watched as the stretcher was loaded off and when I could no longer see her, I suddenly got a phone call."

"Where were you?" Levine asked.

"At the *Café Spritz*. It's just off the dock before you leave all the touristy traps. I was eating and all of a sudden my phone rang. I thought it was Maverick."

"Maverick?"

"Yeah, my buddy on board. He plays the guitar, likes old time theaters."

Levine nodded. "Continue," she said.

The boy looked over at Susan. "Maverick and Rose have the same ringtone, but naturally I thought it was him."

"But it wasn't."

"No, it was her. She wanted to meet me. Said something about always being together and that she didn't want me to get hurt."

"Where did you meet?"

"I told her I was there, at the Café, and she didn't want to have anything to do with that. Said we should meet somewhere farther from the dock, like *Aqua Palms*."

"I know that place!" Susan shrieked, making Jacob jump. "Sorry," she added lamely. "I've just been there, that's all."

"I know," said Jacob, looking down at the table. "I saw you there once."

"You were watching me?"

"Of course. At least at first, when I thought you were the killer."

Susan felt a chill but ignored it. It was just like Jacob to bring her back into the picture and it made her feel uncomfortable. Still, he had seen her at the restaurant.

"And so I told her I would meet her there, but she never showed up. She never came. I haven't heard from her since. She wasn't buried here, either. I went by her mom's place. It was terrible. She blamed me for her daughter's death and other things I'd rather keep to myself." He colored. "You wouldn't believe the rat trap she lives in."

"But you never saw Rose there, at her mother's I mean."

"No, but her mother felt the need to protect me somehow. It was weird, but I guess in some strange way my being there kept her daughter alive."

"But you said she blamed you for her daughter's death."

"That was at first. After a few days I convinced her to look elsewhere. She told me she'd had to send the body off to Florida where the father lived. They were divorced and he took care of all the expenses, including the daughter. I have since wondered if Rose was calling me from the gurney and if, when she got to Florida, still alive and in non-rotting flesh, her father had opened the coffin and she'd jumped out."

"That's silly," Levine said.

"Creepy," Susan offered, "if you'd been the one she'd talked to from the stretcher." Susan paused, wondering what to say next. The thought of Rose in the coffin being shipped to Florida, gave her withering thoughts of losing air and dying before she'd even made it to her destination. But Levine helped her.

"And Henry. What do you know about his whereabouts?"

"Henry?" The boy seemed surprised at the question.

"You don't know?"

The boy shrugged.

"He's missing, you dope!" The exasperation flew from her mouth, but there it was. She looked into Jacob's eyes as deeply as she dared. "Henry's gone!"

End of Her Rope

By that afternoon, Susan had learned Joe's brother, George, and the infamous Jacob Carlson had known each other. Teachers came in all varieties it seemed, and George had tutored Jacob in math in his earlier days when Jacob was still in middle school.

But the surprising information didn't come from George or Jacob. The shock came from Rose's mother, Sarah. They were sitting on the front porch and Susan was beyond worried.

She'd checked the only hangout she knew he'd be at, *Aqua Palms*, and had spent part of the time in the sleazy hotel she'd forever have to live in until they found him. Since Hawaii wasn't Henry's home, no one had any idea where he'd gone, and though they were still looking—Kealoha eyes were red as volcanic ash and Levine was as skittery as an alley cat in a closed in house—Susan was the worst for wear.

She'd had ample opportunity to think about Henry, who he might be with, and what his condition would be like if they didn't find him soon. She imagined he was still alive on the ground somewhere, having walked deliriously from the hospital, or killed and placed underground. She just had to believe he was still alive.

"Jacob is a sweet boy no matter what you think," Sarah was saying now, disturbing Susan's reflective moment. "You should have seen him years ago before he grew up. That George, he could work wonders with Jacob's frail mind. That boy grew in confidence through the years and I'm sure good old George was a part of it."

"Well, good old George is Joe McLean's brother, the man murdered on the ship. Did you know that?"

"I didn't need to know, until now."

"How long ago since you've seen George?"

"George? Well, that's been years, of course. I might be able to help you after all, that is, if they really were brothers.

Susan nodded, but she didn't know. Had the woman already known the men were brothers, earlier than just moments ago?

***

A few hours later, Susan was again at the Honolulu Police Station when she overheard a conversation between Keoloha and his partner, Levine. Seems there was more to George than met the eye.

"Jacob is worried about the old man," said Keoloha.

"Why is that?"

"Well, his brother's death for one; and the way he talked about his brother's wife—you'd think she was still alive or something. As for…"

Keoloha looked in Susan's direction and lowered his voice. Susan didn't hear anything after that and went to visit Jacob. His pre-trial hearing was in a week and she was running out of time.

Jacob had been moved to the local jail and the boy was sitting on a chair in the visiting area when she approached him. The place was noisy, but Jacob didn't seem to notice. He was drumming his fingers on the table. She could see the wheels in his head following suit.

He jumped when he saw her. "Hi," he said, standing up, and then sitting again. "What's up?"

The guard looked them over and walked away.

Susan lowered her voice. "Tell me about George," she said.

"George?"

"George, Joe's brother."

A sparkle lit up Jacob's eyes. "You know him?" he asked.

"I learned all about your math skills."

"Or lack of them." He smiled. "That George, he could teach a one armed bandit to count."

Susan smiled.

"Why do you want to know about George?" he asked.

"Seems he may have something to do with Henry's' kidnapping."

"Old George? He might be great at math, but kidnapping?" A cloud, or was it only a blink, covered Jacob Carlson's left eye. He was silent and looked away from Susan's penetrating gaze.

Jacob seemed uncomfortable and Susan wondered at the strange feeling that was caressing her flesh. "So what do you know?" she asked, the prickly sensation running up her arm and down her back.

"If I tell you, you must keep it a secret," said Jacob. He leaned into the table between them. "George has some mental issues."

"Is that all?" Susan looked into Jacob's eyes. "Are you saying his state of mind would cause him to take Henry? But he's so old. How would he have managed it?"

"Perhaps he has his own flunkies. I hate to rat out on my teacher, but he's different from when I first met him. Changed, you know."

Susan thought about change. And then she thought about all the people she'd met on the island that could have managed such an abduction. What man may have been able to take Henry without detection?

And then her heart gave a leap.

***

With the money she'd been receiving from her new business, Susan bought tickets and boarded the *Aloha*. It was just her luck the cruise line was traveling the islands again, and she hadn't missed her window of opportunity. If Henry was on the ship, she would find him.

She took the only room available, and it didn't have a window. Still, Susan knew why she was taking yet another cruise and a window would cause distraction. She placed her bags on the blue bedspread, clipped her suitcase open, and began to hang up her clothing—the same clothing she had washed multiple times since coming to the islands.

For a moment she thought of Jane, all alone, trying to run the *Hotel Camaro* without her; and then she'd feel at peace. Jane was alright, would be alright until she returned. But when would that be? She'd begun this madness the end of July, now she was into mid-

August. A month of maddening sleuthing was coming to an end; two murders had been committed and a kidnapping with no ransom note had taken place.

It struck Susan then the kidnappers might never have wanted money anyway, but Henry's silence. He must have known something he hadn't shared with her. He must have kept a clue to himself for some reason and the kidnappers had discovered his ruse.

Who was the kidnapper? And was he or she also the murderer? If so, Henry might be dead and she'd lost the opportunity for someone to be in her life again. Perhaps, after all of this, Henry had made his way to the ship alone, but after just having a heart attack?

In amongst all the turmoil, did she want Henry in her life? Did she want to sit with him on the couch as she'd done with Bob and eat junk food? Would Henry want her to have a child like Bob had wanted? But she was nearing forty and had a hard time believing she could have a child now, even if she could get pregnant...

What was she thinking about? If Henry was dead, if she found him rigid in a stateroom or dead cold in the morgue, her dreams of matrimony would all be ended anyway. And she would never see Henry again.

Incognito

The ship was packed this trip, and it was all Susan could do to avoid the crowds while searching for Henry. Henry wouldn't be on the cruise ship list, Susan was sure of that. Besides, how would she get the list if he was?

She was far from friends with Captain Starling, and her best bet was staying on board incognito. She'd purchased a ball cap, which she wore on board, and had colored her brown hair to a wieldy blond. The new haircut fell to her shoulders, and even she had to admit she looked different than her usual self.

Although one insistent thought occupied her mind, Susan had decided while unpacking her clothing for the third time, she'd rule out the obvious places first. It was at the last moment she'd thought of Candace, and wondered if she would assist her. Candace may have access to other rooms Susan could only hope to enter. Would she help?

So it was with mixed feelings that Susan knocked on Candace's cabin door. A young man answered, probably between the ages of 20 and 25. He smiled over at her; his piercing light green eyes blinking at her as if she'd just awakened him.

"Is Candace here?" she asked.

"Why sure." The boy opened the door and ushered her in. Candace was on the bed, the sheet propped up under her chin. "What do you want?" she asked.

"You remember me. Susan. It's Susan."

The girl blinked and got off the bed the sheet around her like a mummy in wraps. The young man ushered her further into the room. Susan was embarrassed.

"You do sound familiar," she said. "Oh, yes, I remember! But you've changed your hair."

"Sorry. I ah...I guess you heard about Rose."

"Yes." The girl sniffed, wiping her nose against the sheet. Her long, dark hair had fallen out of its ponytail and she looked like a Hawaiian goddess standing there, holding up the patterned sheet.

"So, who did it?" she asked.

For the first time Susan surveyed the room. Nothing was in order, and multiple gowns were on the floor along with cups and plates and an assortment of trash.

"That's why I'm here," said Susan. "To find the killer."

"You a cop?" The young man asked. His dark, curly hair fell above his ears.

"Sorry. No. I..."

"Good. Wouldn't want to talk to a cop. What do you want to know?"

Susan was taken aback. "So, did you know Rose, too?"

He laughed. "Everyone knew Rose. When the cops came around and spoke to all of us after her death, we told them about her." He turned to Candace. "But not everything."

"What do you mean, not everything?"

"Want to sit?" The young man with no name offered her a steel chair, but first he knocked off some dirty socks and a soiled T-shirt. Candace flew passed her and into the bathroom and Susan waited for what was sure to be an informative talk.

***

"She what?"

"She had some sort of mental hang-up," the young man said. Susan still didn't know his name and didn't ask him. "Rose thought she was an old woman."

"Because she dressed like one?"

Candace was back from the bathroom. She was wearing a hot pink T-shirt and short white shorts emphasizing her long legs. "It was more than the dressing. She liked to be an old woman. Once I caught her just walking the halls and talking to old men. It creeped me out."

"Maybe she was just leaving or going to the next act and wanted to play the part."

"Maybe. Sometimes she'd just wear the get-up to make life interesting. She said she was practicing for the next show but I didn't believe her."

"Why?"

The young man winked at Candace and the girl blushed. "Oh, maybe it will be alright."

Sitting on the bed opposite, Candace wiped her thin hands against her shorts. "I never would have realized the lie unless I'd seen it for myself. Remember the night that old guy died?"

Susan nodded though her heart thumped.

"Well, I saw them together before that."

"And are you sure it was Rose?"

The young man coughed and wiped his hand through his dark hair. "I was getting on my uniform and had just left my stateroom. She was standing just down the hall and laughing with some old guy. I knew right away it was Rose. She was laughing and hanging on his arm and talking to him about how rich they were. It was strange. Later, at the dance, I was staring at them, wondering what they were going to do next. I was so embarrassed. When Mr. McLean was found murdered on deck, I saw you there, hovering over the guy and thought you'd had something to do with it."

"Me?"

"You were the only one out there other than Rose and that ship guy. But then it occurred to me you had no reason to kill the old coot, but she did."

Susan's skin crawled like so many centipedes. "So why would she kill him?"

"For his money, of course."

"But why would someone kill *Rose*?" Candace asked.

The question tumbled in Susan's mind. It was the same one she'd asked herself over and over again. Was Rose also killed for the money she was beginning to gather from her dead husband, or for something else?

"So what are you going to do?" Candace asked. She blinked over at her boyfriend. His rapt attention was complete.

"I believe a police officer has been abducted and brought aboard. He carries the secret to this mystery and I need your help in finding him," Susan said.

***

It was dark before she met up with Candace and her friend, Robert. They walked hand-in hand and discussed with her down the long hallway what they'd found out about the galley kitchen.

"Everything was empty," shrugged a quiet Candace. "That's good, right?"

The hairs on Susan's body stood on end.

"Thanks, you two. I meant to check the morgue but haven't been able to make it down there. Do you think the two of you could get in?"

"I suppose so," said Candace.

Robert touched her shoulder and squeezed it. Though the gesture didn't hurt, Susan wondered about the young man's honesty. She wondered about Candace, and considered the fact she might have said too much. What if they were both on the up-and-up but she still got hurt?

"I'll go back now," Candace said.

"What did you say you did on board?" Susan asked Robert as Candace left them.

"I'm a steward."

Did Rose ever bring food back to her stateroom that you knew about? Say fish?" she asked.

"Fish? No. But she was one to swindle the wine. She had something going on with the captain..."

"Really! Why didn't you tell me about that before?"

"You mean about the captain or the wine?"

"Both." Susan wasn't sure what it was but the connection had to be important.

***

Susan shuddered. The two had just returned from the ship's morgue to tell her the terrible news. Henry was dead.

KATHRYN ELIZABETH JONES

"I'm so sorry." Huge droplets fell from Candace's brown eyes. Her boyfriend, Robert, had his slim arm around his girl and he didn't appear to want to speak. The warmth in her stateroom had diminished to a cold chill Susan couldn't explain and in that moment she wished she could step outside and throw herself overboard.

In the next instant she changed her decision and turned to her friends, thanked them, and ushered them out of the room. Nothing mattered now. The murder. Anything.

She was awake, no sleep came; her friend's words thundered in her mind until she covered her ears with her hands. She recalled the first time they'd met, in that chill place called the *Hotel Camaro*. She remembered the sugar he was always asking for, and how, even then, she'd thought him a bit strange. Hadn't she just left her husband? Why would she want to be with someone else? When she'd found him dead, and then later discovered he was alive, she'd been so happy. But how happy? Happy enough to make him more than a friend? Happy enough to take him into her life?

What might have happened if she'd answered in the affirmative when he'd asked for her hand in marriage? Would he be dead even now, or would he have taken her somewhere else? Somewhere far beyond mysteries, and killings and death?

Why had she said *no*? She no longer cared how he parted his hair, and that it looked like fish entrails. She didn't care that he was a bit absent minded, had a heart condition and somehow he'd managed to get into scrapes larger than her own. And now, now she was alone again, forever alone.

She would have to say good-bye. Go to the morgue herself and give him a kiss. Say something—anything, tell him she was sorry. That it was wrong of her to turn him down when it would have been easy to say yes. It was the fear keeping her away. The fear of life returning to the first round with Bob. She would do anything to change the first round!

Susan wiped at her eyes, swallowed, and made her way to the morgue. She didn't care if anyone saw her, but she prayed no one would stop her. She would say good-bye, ask for forgiveness, and hope in the deepest part of her being he would forgive her.

Truth

Turning on the light, Susan made her way into the room. It was near midnight. All was quiet. But her mind was playing tricks on her. Would Henry rise when he saw her? Would he somehow, unexplainably, still be alive? She looked in the first vault. Nothing. The second was filled with what appeared to be storage of some kind. The third? A chill ran through her skin as she looked in.

Sure enough there was a man lying in there.

"I'm so sorry!" she screamed inside herself and pulled the sheet from the man's face.

She wasn't sure what she would see. The man she knew she loved, his face a stark white, his lips bluing from death.

What she saw was red hair. A pale face. Closed eyes. A nose much larger than she remembered. Lips. A face. His face? No, it was some other man. Sure, the hair was the same, and the body size, and even the approximate age, but this wasn't, it wasn't Henry!

She'd kissed the man full on the mouth before realizing what she'd done. And then she was laughing, laughing!

She wasn't sure how long she laughed but a short grunt finally caught her attention.

"Excuse me. What are you doing in here?" someone asked.

The place was suddenly lit to full capacity, and Susan stood there, all inadequacies and fears leaving her skin and falling at her feet. What could she say? How could she explain her presence?

The man was in his pajamas and he was rubbing his eyes.

"Who are you?" she asked.

"The attendant here. And you?"

"Oh, I'm just…you know…sick."

"Funny name, Sick. Do you know this man?"

"I thought I did, but no."

"Now I understand the kissing," the man said. "How did you get in here?"

Susan struggled for an answer. "I just came down," she said.

"That's funny…but no matter. Now you know this man isn't a relative, perhaps you can leave so I can get some sleep."

***

"It wasn't Henry!"

"It wasn't?" Candace was rubbing her eyes. Robert was still in bed. It was near 8 a.m., Sunday morning, but Susan just couldn't have waited any longer.

"No."

"Then who?"

"Some other guy with red hair. Can you believe it?"

Candace was quiet. "So, where is he? Maybe they didn't even bring Henry on board."

An expensive miss-step like that made Susan feel—inept. What if he wasn't on board? What if he was already dead somewhere else? But she'd kept in good contact with the police. They hadn't found him as of departure day. Still, the unease was palatable. "You may be right. But I haven't checked the captain's quarters yet."

Candace smiled. "Fortunately, I can get you in there, too," she said.

***

The captain's quarters were elegant, somewhat like royalty, only the furniture lines were straight and the ornamentation kept to a minimum. Susan looked again at the picture of Mr. Joe McLean in full uniform. Younger, surely, but still the man who'd been murdered on the deck of the *Aloha*.

What was his connection to the captain who worked the ship today other than being a fellow officer?

She slipped into the bedroom. The place was picked up and the adjoining living room held photos of the captain's friends and family, she guessed. A small office was part of the spectacle as well a tiny pantry off the kitchen. Susan looked everywhere; under the bed, inside closets, behind doors. Her Henry was not here.

It was upon sneaking back out and walking down the hall that Susan realized her mistake. There would surely be cameras watching the door. And she'd been able to take the key from Candace without question.

***

Candace made no apologies. "Rose used to clean there as well as some of the other staterooms. I made a copy."

Susan smiled; she couldn't help it though she knew if Candace was caught she'd probably lose her job.

"What about the cameras?" Susan asked.

"I have a friend in security."

Susan blinked. "You must have cared about Rose," she said, though her thoughts were on different issues, namely, who Candace really was to wield such power on such a large ship.

"I knew her for a long time," said Candace, looking over at her companion. "She was my sister, after all."

"Your sister?"

"Sorry I didn't tell you before; I just had to be sure of some things first."

"Like what?"

"Like, you trusted me to tell you the truth. I wanted to see you in action myself."

***

It was Monday, and they would be leaving Maui for Hilo at 6. Fortunately, some of the clues were starting to materialize, but finding Henry? How was she ever going to find him? The morgue was vacant of his presence, as was the captain's quarters...she'd even checked the kitchen, the various decks and eating spots—as if somehow he'd be propped up against a ship's wall just waiting for her.

She might have laughed, but it wasn't funny. Nothing was funny.

Perhaps he wasn't here after all. But then again, she hadn't checked the entire ship. Where else could you hold a man against his wishes?

A stateroom...

The thought of Henry being tied down in some cabin somewhere made her wince. She could almost feel the tight ropes against his flesh, the gag in his mouth preventing speech. The captor, pacing the room, wondering what to do next...

And then a thought occurred to her, and it seemed for a time Susan was drifting across the sea, the blue waves cooling her brow. She had to relax, had to think...

Jacob had a friend working on the ship. What was his name? She thought about the young man, cooped up in his small cabin, a guitar in hand. Maverick. That was his name and if he was still friends with Jacob he could have easily done Jacob's bidding when it came to kidnapping Henry. But why?

Was that the only way to keep Henry quiet, or was something else brewing Susan had no clue about?

Rushing to Maverick's room, Susan knocked on the door. No answer. She stood there for some moments wondering what to do when the thought occurred to her that Candace might know. But she was already working at the infirmary—would be for most of the day. She could ask Robert, the boyfriend, he might know.

Susan walked up numerous hallways searching for him. The ship was a bit rocky and she had to hold on to the side rail to keep from falling. She hesitated to knock on the doors, but as she watched various workers going in and out of the rooms she was relieved when she found Robert leaving one near the far end.

He smiled when he saw her. "How's it going?" he asked.

Susan shushed him with her hand and directed him back to the room. "What is it?" he asked again.

"What do you know about Maverick?"

"The guitar player?" He looked her straight in the eyes. "You didn't hear it from me," he said. "Promise."

"Promise what?"

"That whatever I tell you, you won't bring it back to me."

Susan nodded.

"That guy is a real creep-o. C-R-E-E-P-O."

"Why?"

He leaned in. It reminded Susan of Jacob's posture at the jail. "He used to date Candace. I never liked the guy and told Candace she needed to get rid of him. And one day she finally did…"

"Why didn't you like him?"

"Promise?"

"Sure, I said I promised."

"That day Candace saw Rose with the dead guy—before he was dead—I also saw Maverick with Rose. And they were doing more than holding hands. She was in her old lady getup, but the guy didn't seem to notice. He actually seemed to like it. It creeped me out then just as it does now. Candace told me never to mention it again. She feels like a fool for ever liking him."

"She must have been mad at Rose, though."

"Hardly," Robert added. "She was grossed out. Candace was worried about Rose after that and wondered if we should say anything to the doctor. Soon after the old guy was murdered. And another weird thing..." Robert wiped his hair from his eyes. "Maverick changed rooms after that; he's in a suite now, and pretty much keeps to himself. Since Rose's death he keeps himself pretty cloistered. It's strange, too. He leaves for moments at a time, does his gig at night, but never associates with any of us."

"Maybe he's depressed," said Susan, taking the boy's arm. "Show me where he's staying."

***

The guitar player's hair was either wet or greasy. He leaned around the door frame as before, his blond locks flapping against the door. "What do you want?" he hissed.

In that moment Susan had a reality check. The boy probably didn't know her from Adam, and since her hair color had changed maybe he wouldn't remember her. She didn't speak.

"Sorry," she managed to mumble behind her hand.

The door was slammed shut and Susan walked away, her hands shaking. If that boy was holding her Henry, the worst choice she could make would be to ask if he'd seen him. She was so stupid! Better to come to his room at night when he was at the gig playing, find Henry, and take him back to her quarters.

She might have laughed to herself if she wasn't sure Henry was in that room, tied up to Maverick's bed or shoved in the closet. She'd heard nothing when the boy had opened the door. Was her Henry in that room?

Sure it was odd, almost...unbelievable, but there was nowhere else to look. The connection was there. He was Jacob's friend and they had worked together. He was young enough to take her Henry, especially from the hospital where Henry was weak and healing. Oh, her dear Henry! He just had to be in that room!

The Room

The show began at 9, and so Susan waited until 9:15 before entering Maverick's room. The key was easily managed from Candace, and Susan passed the time before entering the cabin by pacing her own floor.

What if he wasn't in there? What if she found someone else? What if she found nothing? Then she'd be no closer to discovering Henry's whereabouts than she was now. No loss, other than time.

She realized he could be dead and any effort would prove fruitless. She realized her Henry might be somewhere else, a place where she'd never find him. She didn't know the islands. She had no idea where he'd be, and neither did the police.

A tear creased her left eye, but she brushed it away. It was 9:15.

Maverick's new place was on the lower deck, just below the shops and fairly close to the infirmary. She wondered if the camera Candace had promised would be pointed in another direction at about that time. She placed the key in the lock and turned the knob.

She entered, creeping at first, and then insistently when not a sound came from inside the room. She flipped on the light. The room was much larger than the one Maverick had shared with Jacob and sported a window with a lifeboat view. Surveying the main room she noticed a desk near the window with a television set above it, a large bed, and a place for sitting near the window. A door to the bathroom was to her right. She clicked the switch on and went inside.

The place was immaculate and small enough to hold only one person at a time. The shower was empty and the place where she was standing held a place for washing and a toilet. And something else.

Taped to the toilet bowl's back was a small cloth bag; something that could be easily missed if one wasn't looking for it. Susan bent to open the white bag, then filled her hand with sparkling jewels. She was distracted for only a minute, fingering the jewels in almost every color of the rainbow, as if they were her own. Replacing the jewels and pushing the bag into her pocket, she turned off the light switch and walked back into the room nearer the window.

She was the stupidest cop on the planet, a fake cop in pretend mode. The place was empty and held a single suitcase propped up on the seating area. Some thin mints were already on the pillow and two beach towels were stacked on a small table in front of the seating area.

Another tear slipped outside her left eye as she stood looking out at the lifeboat. Boy, what a terrible view. No trees, no ocean, just a lifeboat on the other side. How much view did one need as an artist? A lot possibly. And then Susan did a double-take, the view would be important and somehow refreshing, but even the performers didn't get that.

She wiped her cheeks and turned, intent on leaving the room, when she heard it, a slight scuffle, a shift from under the bed.

Rats, they probably have rats here, she thought, and continued to the door. The noise met her ears again. It was slight, like a small mouse, a small something, trying to get her attention, but suddenly Susan realized whatever it was it knew she was there.

She decided to check. It wasn't like her to spy out small vermin, but something about the noise intrigued her, made her pull up the white bed cover and take a peek.

That's when she noticed the missing mattress. And underneath the blue bedcover, taped tightly to the frames sides so it wouldn't fall through, a sheet, and underneath that, more blankets, stacked on the floor at both sides. Not surprisingly, it was the toes she saw first scraping against the suitcase. Feet! Feet underneath the bed!

Scooting one side of the blankets away and throwing them to the side, Susan looked in.

A face peered over at her.

"Henry, Henry, is that you?"

The body was still except for the toe twitching.

Susan reached for Henry. He was still wearing the clothes he'd been taken in. His hair was matted and his face unshaven. She pulled, tugging at his arms and legs until minutes later, he'd been extricated from beneath the bed. Only then could she see him fully.

He didn't speak, just stared up at her. He was a mess. He smelled terrible, too, like something sweet, but decaying. His face was pale, like chalk, and his clothes smelled like alcohol...and sweat.

Henry blinked.

Instinctively, she reached for her cell phone stored in her back pocket.

***

"He looks almost...dead," Candace said.

She was right, of course, and as Robert reached down to lift Henry into his arms, Susan realized he may have lost some weight, but so little she would never have been able to manage lifting him alone. Henry's eyes were closed now and as Susan and Candace gathered up Henry's feet, Susan thought of all of the reasons she loved him.

Susan turned off the light and shut the door and together they carried Henry down the hall. A few strange looks were given in their behalf as they took Henry to Susan's room and laid him on the bed. Robert packed some pillows behind Henry's head at Candace's request, propping him up. Susan retrieved a cold washcloth from the bathroom and Candace checked Henry's pulse.

"I think I know what's going on," she said, "but we need to get him to the ship's infirmary."

Henry's eyes opened. "No..." he said, deliriously.

He closed his eyes again and Candace turned to the door. "I'll get some supplies from the infirmary and be right back." She was gone then, and Susan couldn't do anything but wipe her beloved's brow.

"We're going to get you well," she said.

He nodded, slightly, and closed his eyes again.

The moment was silent, but the silence didn't last. "What's that stale smell?" Robert asked, breaking Susan's thoughts of Henry. "It seems to be coming from...him."

"I noticed it, too." The smell was more than sweat and with a start Susan realized she'd smelled this odor before; in her stateroom when she'd first arrived on board, in Candace's room when Rose was still alive and at George's house on Maui. For the first time, the scents gathered into one and flew connected inside her brain.

She didn't say anything to Robert though, but tried to focus on Henry.

In moments Candace had returned. But she had no medical supplies with her.

"So where are the meds?" Robert asked, taking Candace by the arm.

Candace looked shook up, as if she'd had a confrontation of some kind. "We'll just keep him upright. We have to keep him awake. We have to keep him awake!"

Susan turned to Henry. "Henry?" she asked.

"What?" he moaned, opening his eyes.

"You have to stay awake!"

"Why?"

"Why, Candace, why?" The thought that she had no idea what Henry was going through made Susan feel even weaker. What does he have? What's going on?"

Candace was pale. "I think he has alcohol poisoning. All we can do is keep him upright, just in case, and keep him awake. If he sleeps for too long he may go into a coma."

***

Susan's tears had dried on her face, but by the following day Henry was speaking more than a few slurred sentences.

"I'm so glad you found me," he said.

Susan was alone with him. It was Tuesday morning and her two confidants had returned to their own stateroom to get some sleep.

"I couldn't do anything but find you," she said, moping his brow. It was the one thing she knew how to do. "Do you need to get up...for anything?" she asked.

"Actually, yes. The bathroom?"

"It was good news and Susan was pleased. She walked with him to the small bathroom. He looked at her, his eyes still a bit weepy. "I think I can do the rest."

With the door shut Susan heard some tinkling in the toilet. "I'm going to take a shower," Henry said. "And then we can talk."

With the water spraying, Susan still rooted herself at the door. She listened for anything. A cough. A fall. A yell, but in a few moments the water was shut off and she could hear Henry stepping out of the shower. "Do you mind if I use your toothbrush?" he asked. "I'll get you another."

"You'd better," she sang from the other side of the door.

She could hear a small laugh from Henry and then the turning of the faucet. Still standing at the door, she waited, wondering what Henry would tell her, wondering how she would respond, but mostly, what they would be doing next to catch the killer.

"Do you mind if I use your bath robe?"

Susan realized Henry had no clothes to change into, and probably hadn't managed to purchase any on the ship since he'd been taken against his will. She didn't dare leave him.

"That's fine," she said, hoping the bath robe would fit around him. He opened the door and stepped out, a fine fish, Susan thought, eyeing his wet hair; the way his leg hair flattened against his legs. He walked over to the bed and sat down, pulling the robe around him. It was white and had yellow daisies at the collar. She'd had the robe for years, when she'd first met and married Bob.

Henry blushed. "Thanks," he said.

"No problem. How are you feeling?"

"Pretty out of it, unlike yesterday. You wouldn't believe the stuff I was spitting up. Gray."

"Candace says you were drugged."

"Candace?"

"You remember? Rose's friend."

"Oh. So she was here?"

"Yep. Along with her friend, Robert. If it wasn't for Candace I think I would have gone out of my mind. She's a nurse."

"I thought she worked in housekeeping."

"Nope."

Henry smiled, but his face looked weary.

111

"Lean back and get some rest," she said, trying to help him by propping him up against the starched white pillows. She kept her eyes averted from the possible opening up of the robe.

Once positioned, Henry asked for a drink of water. She brought it to him, thinking of the trouble she was now in – now that Maverick was probably looking all over the ship for him.

***

A day later, Henry was on his feet. They were docking in Kona but Susan had taken extra care in making sure Henry was never left alone. She'd ordered in and hadn't left his side for two days. His coloring was returning and Susan knew he was feeling better. His appetite had even picked up, but she hadn't pushed him about the kidnapper, wanting Henry to improve first.

Still, it looked like Susan wouldn't have to wait much longer.

"Why didn't you get a room with a view?" Henry asked now, reaching for the space that might have been a deck. Instead, he pressed his hand against a cream painted wall and watched her.

"I got on board at the last minute. The place was pretty booked and I had to take what was left."

He smiled, and brushed his other hand through his red hair. "Well, you probably haven't had time to do any vacationing," he said. His eyes darkened. "I'm surprised he hasn't found me yet."

"He, who?" Susan asked, her heart pounding.

He blinked. "I thought you knew."

"I only know someone brought you here against your will. I'm guessing, Maverick."

"Maverick." Henry tried to smile.

"So Maverick kidnapped you and brought you to his room? For what purpose?"

Henry touched his heart. "I guess I did a stupid thing. I was walking the hospital grounds early Saturday morning when he found me. I was pretty weak and went to sit down on a lounge chair when I felt this tight grip around my arm. I didn't have much strength to fight him with; still, he's a pretty strong guy. It didn't take much to walk me out of there. He even got me into the car at the hospital without anyone noticing. It still makes me angry. He had the whole kidnapping planned out. What day is it?"

"August 8th."

"Holy cow. I've been under that bed for almost three days!"

"Any longer and you'd be dead."

"No doubt," Henry said. He tightened the tie at his waist, blushed, and walked to the other side of the room. "You'll need to wash my clothes or find me some new ones. Maybe Robert has something..."

"I'll ask."

"But keep everything else a secret. They may be involved."

Susan hesitated. "Really?"

Henry's head bobbed. "Hang tight for now. Did you bring your phone?"

Susan handed him her cell phone and he proceeded to dial the police station.

SUNNY SIDE-UP

Long Shot

"So he's up and walking around?"

Susan nodded. "He needs some clothes."

Robert reached within the closet he was now sharing with Candace and pulled out some jeans and a turquoise T-shirt. "Here," he said, handing them to her. "My shoes probably won't fit."

"That's okay. I just need to get him out of my bathrobe."

"Your bathrobe?" the boy winked.

Susan tried to remain calm. "He just needs to look halfway presentable on board the ship." She made a motion to leave the room but Robert stopped her. "So who took him anyway?" he asked. "Maverick?"

"He hasn't told me," she lied, hoping the lie was convincing. "He still seems a bit out of it."

Robert smiled slightly, and brushed his hand on her shoulder. "But we found him in Maverick's room..."

The revelation should have soothed her, but as she left the room with Candace asleep on the top bunk, all she could think about was the strange tingling sensation traveling up her back.

***

Once dressed, Susan wondered about their next step. She watched as Henry combed his hair. He was brushing his teeth again, and reaching for a washcloth. "I feel as if gray stuff is coming out of my skin in buckets," he said. "The police want us to stay tight. They'll be entering the ship when we dock at Kauai tomorrow morning. Then they can put Maverick into custody."

Susan's heart sank. "What if he's already left the ship? I mean he must know by now you're with me. He could be on Maui. Or he might have even stepped out in Hilo. Do you think he's on Kona?"

"Could be..."

"Sorry..." Susan told Henry. "I honestly was more concerned about your health than watching for the kidnapper."

"That's good of you." He turned to her and watched her for a moment before continuing. "Really good of you, but we have to be open to the possibility Maverick discovered I was missing soon after I was taken. He may have left, sooner or later, or he may yet be on board. Still, a day wouldn't have gone by without him checking up on me – such as his checking up on me was."

Susan could only guess at what Henry had gone through. She imagined no food for days, plenty of drugs, and perhaps only water to sustain him.

"I'm sorry," she offered. "If he's already left the ship, what will we do?"

Henry smiled. "We have a few short hours left on Kona. I heard some talk about a jewel shipment being delivered. Thinking I was going to die anyway, Maverick didn't hold back on his future plans. If he's ashore...I know exactly where he'll be hiding."

Susan fingered the small bag of jewels in her pocket.

***

The air was as moist as the back of her neck, but Susan's lengthening hair was pulled in a ponytail, her bright eyes searching for clues.

Unfortunately, she didn't see any.

Maverick wasn't on board – even his guitar was gone and his clothes and other belongings were thrown to the side of the bed.

She'd blundered yet again, but she couldn't worry about that now. All she could think about was Henry and the teen that, at any moment, could come thundering behind them with a gun.

For this reason, Henry had finally been given a gun by the police before they'd embarked on the last cruise. As for now, Maverick's room had come up empty by the two of them except for an old theater magazine and various toiletries. That's when Susan, hopeful she had finally done something noteworthy, had revealed the small bag.

Minutes later she and Henry were at the Kona Movie Theater just off of North Queens and Henry was scrounging through old theater remnants hoping to find the remainder of jewels he'd heard Maverick speak about as he'd lain drugged underneath the bed.

The room was classic in its ornaments: gilded ceilings, draperies in red, seats cushioned in the latest crushed velvet of the season. The room was large, and the owner, a creepy man with bulging red eyes and an equally round belly, had met them at the door.

"This theater has been closed for years," he said. "What you'd be a-wanting?"

Susan recalled, not with fondness, the outside of the building before they'd been let in. The place, such as it was, was falling apart. The theater's blue and white facing sported a pink and white sign near the roof area: "Kona" it read, as if somehow the addition was needed when the words, "Kona Theater" were boldly printed at either side. The bushes were tall, and the trash high; some of the windows had even been boarded.

"Just a short look," said Henry, giving the man his best smile, and hovering his police badge over the man's eyes.

She coughed, and as the dust wafted to her eyes, she watched as her Henry rummaged through boxes, bins and underneath carpets.

"Check that wall," he ordered.

A wall with partially covered paper was torn from the surface, revealing cement. She touched it, the coolness feeling its way into her pores. "This wall?" she asked, and in just that moment she heard a thump from the other side.

She turned. Henry was still searching. She could see his red hair, his hands maneuvering between broken down chairs and carpet remnants.

"Henry?"

The silence on the other side of the wall was deafening. When Henry didn't answer she turned and followed the walkway to the adjoining room. It was sickeningly dark, and Susan brushed her hands against the hallway, feeling her way to the other side.

Around the corner she turned, only to be met by another open room and what appeared to be more chairs and boxes. Someone blinked at her. It was the old man, a flashlight in his hand. "What you doing in here, Missy?" he asked.

"Just thought I'd look..."

Her trembling hands reached for the wall only to meet up with the man's hand. "I'm just cleaning in here," he said. "Going to be renting the place out. You folks interested?"

Susan blinked. Hadn't Henry shown the old man his badge? Why would the geezer think they were trying to rent the place?

"It will take some work," he said. "Old lighting, old furniture, old equipment. Still, what about an old theater? We used to have fine dancers when I was young."

"Sorry, sir. I'm going back to the other room."

A firm hand grasped her left arm. "I'll walk you back."

Susan thanked the man, but there was a crawling sensation underneath her skin. In moments, the old man had left her and she was looking down at Henry.

"You won't believe what I found," he said, when the old man was out of ear-shot.

"What?"

He patted his pocket. "Better to wait." With a start, he led her to the outer door.

Outside the building the old man stood waiting. "So, what do you think?" he asked.

"We're not interested," Henry replied, and Susan followed him back to the car.

Once inside, Henry reached inside his jean pocket. I figured it was no use continuing the search," he said, lifting a bag to her eyes.

Susan couldn't believe it.

Robert had helped her find Henry, though he still might be a part of the jewel robberies. And if Robert, then probably Candace. Rose was dead and so was Mr. Joe McLean. And now Maverick was missing. But two bags of jewels had been found.

**

"A jewel thief, huh?" They were back in Honolulu, at police headquarters, and Kealoha and Levine were pacing. "And how do you propose the jewels are mixed in with the murder fiasco?"

Henry was sitting. He looked pale again and Susan was worried about his heart. They'd spent half an hour by plane from Kona to Maui, a bit longer to Honolulu, but the flights had disturbed him. After this double murder investigation was solved, she'd tell him the truth about her feelings and he'd take her away from all of this for good.

"Consider a young woman who marries an old man fully intent on making the money she wants at his death," Henry began, "only the man is murdered by someone else before her plan can be put into effect. Rose discovers there is also money to be made in jewels and begins searching for those who are stealing them. If she can get her hands on the jewels, why worry about the old man?" Henry began.

"She meets up with Maverick after leaving her relationship with Jacob and discovers there is more to him than meets the eye. Though she doesn't let him in on her little scheme, Maverick discovers the lie – he thinks she's in love with him (he also knows about her double identity) and kills her so she'll never reveal the secret of his jewel smuggling..."

"...Consider that Mr. McLean discovered what was going on. He found out his wife had married him for his money and in the interim figured out she was also involved in jewel theft using the *Aloha* as transport. When he discovers Maverick has his hands dirty, he is killed as is Rose after that..."

"And we also know," offered Susan, "George, Joe's brother, is connected to both murders."

All three stared at her as if she'd gone crazy. Sure, it wasn't enough that Henry had laid everything else out for them; all she had to do was mention one clue and she'd get her hands slapped.

"Think of it. The smell connects all three."

"What smell?" Henry asked. He peered behind him, almost as if he'd forgotten she was there.

"The smells! The same 'someone' was in my stateroom before I entered it. That strange smell like dirt and weird sweat, kind of acrid, you know like you smelled when I discovered you."

Henry swallowed. She could see his Adam's apple bobbing. "What are you saying?"

"Consider this." Susan smiled, she just couldn't help it. "Someone was in my room when I wasn't there – same smell. And while we were at George McLean's house, I smelled that same smell. What if George had something to do with his brother's murder? And if Joe's murder, what about Joe's wife? It was obvious he didn't like her."

They all stared at her as if she was a ghost.

"Think of it. George is angry because his brother is the rich one. He even finds a younger woman to marry. George knows this. He also knows the woman is no good. He finds a way to get rid of her after the death of his brother..."

"Seems a bit farfetched to me," said Henry, still looking at her, his blue eyes searching and wondering."

"Still, she does have a point," broke in Kealoha. He fingered his golden ring.

"Especially since the brother tutored Jacob in math," Susan added.

"He did what?" Henry stood. He peered down at her from his full height. It made Susan feel uncomfortable and like a bug on a windshield.

"Uh, Sarah, Rose's mother told me. George was Jacob's math coach. I thought you knew."

"When did you talk with Sarah?" Henry was still leaning over Susan. This time he found her a chair.

***

The new facts brought a new stir to the police department in Honolulu, and Susan was suddenly and without question taken seriously for the first time; at least, that's how it appeared to her. Jacob was re-questioned, with her in sight, and another visit was made to Rose's mother, Sarah.

The connections between them were getting thicker and it was all Susan could do to keep her brain from racing ahead and making her crazy.

That night she and Henry had another meal at *Aqua Palms* and they discussed this connection in-between bites of loco moco. Life was a bit loco when she thought about it. Could Joe really have been killed by his brother? And what about Mr. McLean's wife? Why didn't he like her? Was it really about her age, or had he uncovered something else?

"So what do you think about George? I think we need to see him again and discuss his involvement in his brother's affairs," Susan asked.

"Do you think he will fess up?" queried Henry. "I mean, he doesn't want us to know he had anything more than a bystander relationship with his brother."

"I know." Susan took a bite of rice. She hoped she'd be able to get the loco moco down without too much trouble. "But what if we could prove George was getting booze – for free?"

Henry smiled and took a bite of his own loco moco. "The man could be buying it for all we know. Besides..." here Henry hesitated, and his face paled. "Didn't Candace have the same sort of smell in her room?"

For a moment Susan's mind went blank. She tried to replace the scene in Candace's room, the couple of times she had been there, with the smell she and Henry had both noticed. But that would mean the person in her stateroom was either Candace or George, and it couldn't have been George unless he was on the cruise ship without either of them knowing about it.

No, that couldn't be. Weren't the police watching George's house like a hawk? Candace was the only one who had access to both Joe and his wife. And if she was working along with her new boyfriend, Robert, then the two of them were in this together and Henry was right.

"Let's say Robert and Candace have smuggled jewels for awhile, until Rose catches them. They kill her to keep their secret. But what about Joe McLean? There must be two murderers. The first is someone else; maybe George, the second is either Jacob or his friends Candace and Robert, or Maverick. We know Maverick took you. So what if all of them are working together?" she asked.

"That makes sense. So they are found out by Rose and one of them ends her life the same way they tried to end mine. Except I wonder if they were really trying to end mine."

Susan was confused. "Why not?" she asked. She could no longer eat. Half of the loco moco sat on her plate, cooling.

"What if they just wanted me out of the way for awhile?"

"Away from what?"

"The precinct and all those we've been speaking with in Honolulu. The snooping around the cruise ship. Consider the places of the strange smells. First we have your room on the *Aloha*. And then we have Candace's room on the *Aloha*. Last, we have George's house. But he hasn't been on the *Aloha* that we know of. So that makes two distinct places – not including my person – where the same smell has been discovered.

Less than Friendly Visits

"What?! I didn't kill my brother, and I didn't kill his stupid wife!"

The man was frantic and a bit lunatic. He wouldn't even sit. "Sure, I didn't like his wife...she was too young for him, but that doesn't mean I killed her!"

"Tell us again what you didn't like." Henry was still sitting and so was she, but his eyes were taut on the man who might have murdered his own brother.

"She was made up, any man with eyes could see that. Any man would be able to tell she was dressed up as an old woman; faking her voice."

Henry's eyes lit up. "How did you know she was faking her voice?"

"Well, it would change, you know? She would have the voice down and then she'd forget and use her own voice, stuff like that. But I couldn't convince Joe she was a fake. He said he loved her."

Henry nodded then plunged in for the question that was on both of their minds. "And what about Jacob, the boy behind bars? You say you've never heard of him."

"That's right." The old man turned away. Susan could see two distinct grease spots where the man had wiped his hands, and the place still smelled of sweat and other unmentionables.

"But Rose Anderson's mother, Sarah, says otherwise. She says you tutored Jacob in math."

"The woman is lying," the man spit. Susan looked away for a moment and her eyes traveled to the window. A large palm tree stood at the outskirts.

"So, you have no knowledge of Jacob, the boy who will be accused of murder unless you speak up?"

"That boy couldn't hurt a fly! He's as mild as...a baby kitten."

"So, you *do* know him."

The man's face paled. "Okay, I know him, and he's too much of a weakling to do anything – especially kill someone. Sure, he puts out this tough exterior, but I know his true heart. It would make your hair curl to know some of the things he'd have other folks do just so he wouldn't have to do it himself."

Susan nodded at Henry. She prodded him to go on.

"Like what?"

The man hesitated. "I should be keeping this a secret. I promised."

"Promised who?" Henry asked.

"Rose's mother. It was just like her to take in stray cats...stray people. I promised her I wouldn't try to implicate Jacob any more than he already was."

"But she told us you tutored Jacob."

"I know that," the man spit. He remained where he was. "It was a mistake...a mistake..."

"So why the big secret?" Susan asked.

He turned to her, his eyes glaring. "Wouldn't you like to know."

Susan sat waiting, but George remained quiet. "So I tutored the boy," he finally admitted, "but the creep showed his thanks by taking off without paying his dues." He looked straight into the eyes of Susan. "He forgot to pay me."

"Couldn't have been that much."

"No, but that's beside the point. I thought I was teaching an honest boy. Time came for payment and he never showed up. I heard about him recently when he was put in jail and Sarah asked me to keep quiet about it. She's a friend so I kept quiet."

"So what would Jacob ask others to do?" The question was repeated because George hadn't answered it.

"Steal for him. He began getting into trouble and it was all Sarah could do to keep him straight."

"So you've known Sarah for a long time."

George sat. A waft of stench filled Susan's nose and made her cough.

"Roses mother and I... were a couple once, but I couldn't handle the daughter. She was a strange sort of gal, always wanting some new adventure, thinking I could help her mom pay for it. I think she's crazy, but now that she's gone, I just tell Sarah her girl is better off *in the great beyond*. I tell her, her daughter is happier now she doesn't have to work so hard at making people like her. The girl couldn't be herself."

"Why do you say that?"

George wiped at his pants. "She was always pretending to be someone else. It made my hair curl, just like it does now just talking about it."

Susan thought about the old woman garb that Rose wore, but remained silent. It was evident to her that George had not yet discovered Rose was the woman he didn't like – Sylvia Mclean.

$$***$$

"Isn't it strange George hasn't yet discovered the true identity of Sylvia McLean?" Susan asked.

Back in the car, Henry drove to the jail to talk with Jacob. His pre-trial hadn't gone well, now he was looking at the full-blown experience. It made Susan sick that a young man would have to deal with the situation, such as it was, and she was determined to ease the experience as much as possible, even if the boy was the murderer of Rose, though she doubted it.

If George was correct, the boy didn't have it in him. Perhaps he was at the wrong place at the wrong time, or maybe he hadn't had the courage to kill Rose himself and so had gotten someone else to do it for him. Someone like Maverick would be able to do the trick.

$$***$$

On Thursday, while the cruise ship docked at Kauai, both Candace and Robert were brought into police headquarters in Honolulu and questioned. Maverick was still on the loose. Susan got squirrel like looks from Candace and silence from Robert. The words, *after all we've done to help you?* kept coursing inside her brain until it was all she could do to think straight.

125

Candace's room on the *Aloha* had been searched. Rose's portable player was found hidden behind the wardrobe. A stash of liquor had been discovered inside the shower, inside the closet and under the bed of Candace's room. The police had listened to the music without her and found only music, but the room was still being searched at last word. The booze was another story and a bad one.

"We were storing them."

"For whom?" Henry was across the table, and Candace sat across from him, her dark hair swept up into a messy bun. She didn't look well and smelled worse. Susan sat in the back corner and promised she'd remain quiet.

"For those who wanted it?" Henry said. He'd just asked Candace who she'd purchased the alcohol for. "Like crew members?"

Candace smiled. " They liked the price. Free. We'd steal it and everyone was quiet."

"From where?"

"The hold, of course, down by the storage."

"How did you get it without being seen?"

"We'd gather a few bottles at request of the galley, and take a couple for ourselves. The gathering was easy. In time we had a whole slew of them."

At last count the police had gathered 50 bottles from the room.

"Work is tough, you know? We needed some way to cool off."

Henry leaned in. It wasn't like him to lean in unless he had something important to say. And now it came. "Did the captain know about this? The wine steward?" he asked.

The girl hesitated. "Not sure."

"Strong rules about booze are a part of every cruise ship. You think you can just take what you want for the picking?"

The girl was silent.

"Tell me about Rose," he finally asked.

The girl moved her tiny feet from under the chair and placed them in front of her.

"She was a good sister, and then, she changed."

"How?"

"Oh, she wanted more sister-ship than I had inside me." The girl moaned. "She wanted Robert."

"What was wrong with Jacob? With Maverick?"

She paused. "Jacob was a wimp; Maverick, a leach. Neither would be a part of all she wanted to do and be in life."

"Like what?"

The girl reached a hand through her hair. "Oh, she wanted to act. She wanted to earn lots of money. She felt lost in the big ship and wanted out."

"How did she want out?"

The girl shrugged. "I never knew, for sure, but I had my suspicions."

"What did you suspect?"

Susan looked past the girl and to Henry's eyes. From her angle she could see every nuance of feeling. Henry was close to receiving an answer. She could feel it.

"She killed the old men traveling on the cruise the ship; except this time, it didn't work out so well for her."

"Why do you say that?"

"She'd marry a guy, an old one, and it was months later before I heard he was dead. I kept track."

"How many?"

Chills like a giant wave reached into Susan's heart. She waited.

"Five at last count. This last time though, was different."

"In what way?"

Candace was silent for a moment, and then Susan watched as the girl put her legs back underneath her chair. "She'd just married the guy. Just one day and she was excited, you know, like usual. I always knew when it would come. She would honeymoon on the ship and then a few months would pass. In time she'd return and they'd hire her back on. I could never figure that part out."

"What was to figure out?"

"You know. You work your job for a few weeks, leave the ship for a few months, and then return without having worked your job for that time. If I'd done it, I wouldn't have been able to get my old job back."

"And she didn't know you suspected anything?"

"I'm not sure."

127

"So why haven't you discussed this with the police?"

"I couldn't do that."

"Why?"

Candace placed her hands on the table. "I was stealing, you know?"

***

Robert was a lot less open. He answered every question, curtly, as if Henry was the one being questioned and he was the one who was innocent.

He shrugged.

"You're unsure of why you stored the liquor."

"To drink it, I guess."

"No other reason?"

"To share it."

"How much did you know Rose?"

"A little."

"And?"

"She was a looker but I wasn't interested."

"But she was interested in you."

"I suppose so."

"And?"

"Well, she was strange, that's all. Jacob and Maverick had troubles with her, too."

"What kind of troubles?"

"Neither of them trusted her, though Jacob never liked the old woman garb like Maverick."

"So why all the booze?"

"I told you. To drink and to share."

"No other reason?"

"Not that I can think of."

"Who did you share the alcohol with?"

"Lots of folks."

"Like who?"

"Oh, Rose...sometimes we'd take some out to George." The boy blushed.

"You mean George, the brother of Joe McLean who was killed?"

Robert nodded but remained silent.

"Why would you do that?"

"It kept him quiet."

Now Susan's heart thundered. She couldn't sit still.

"Why would George need to be kept quiet?"

"He had an addiction for liquor. He also knew what was going on, on the *Aloha*."

Henry was silent and it occurred to Susan he waited for an answer. The boy was squirming in his seat; he didn't want to share what was inside. But Henry waited. Finally Robert spoke.

"Okay, you guys will find out anyway..." He brushed his fingers through his hair. "George knew jewels were being smuggled onto the *Aloha*. He promised he'd keep quiet as long as we kept him stocked up."

"And the smuggling? Were you a part of that?"

The boy blushed again. "Sort of."

Henry waited.

"Look, Candace was dealing in stolen gems far longer than I was. When I met her I found out all about it and started to join in. You know, going into homes and getting the stuff. But I wasn't as slick as Jacob was. He could reach through a panel and find stuff hidden."

Susan thought of the secret panel at the *Hotel Camaro*. The one she'd once hidden her treasures in, and then turned her attention back to Robert.

"I know I've been stealing, but I would never hurt anyone – especially Rose."

"Do you have any idea who might have murdered her?"

"Well, Jacob couldn't have done it..."

"You know the ship cameras show he entered Rose's room an hour before her death," said Henry.

Robert looked surprised. "Well, Maverick was the heavy man. He would do all of the scary stuff. Take yourself for example..."

Henry leaned in. "Then you knew I'd been kidnapped."

"Of course I knew. But we had to do it," Robert offered.

"Why?"

"You were too close to the answers, and Maverick suggested we take you from the hospital before you got your strength back.

The good news is you made it easy for us, sitting outside. It almost made me sick when I found out. I almost laughed..." The boy looked into Henry's eyes and continued: "We thought you knew all about the jewel heists and the alcohol stealing and we didn't want you to take us in."

"So you were all involved? You, Rose, Maverick, Jacob and Candace?"

"Yep. And George too, only he didn't steal anything, just kept the secret so we could keep making money." The boy shrugged. "I know what you're thinking. How does one pull off stealing liquor from a ship that accounts for everything? I wondered about that for a long time, it just seemed, well, too easy. Funny thing, though. Rose must have figured something out we didn't know about. I have always wondered why she was murdered so close to the murder of Joe McLean."

"Why is that?"

"I knew Rose dressed up; all of us did, though we didn't let her in on the secret. Rose was strange and we didn't want her to lash out at any one of us. But something must have happened, she must have seen something to cause her death, though I wonder how it connects with the death of that old guy."

Sunny Side-Up

It was late and Susan tried to sleep. It was no use. All of the facts bubbled inside of her with no way out. It was too late to talk to Henry and she had no one else to talk to.

When she couldn't hold her thoughts any longer she reached for Henry. He shared her bed, but they were still as platonic as the sky was blue. No kiss. Little hand holding. A look. A slight caress across the hand. Nothing else.

"W-what?" he mumbled as she shook him. He'd purchased a pair of pajamas and his long sleeve drifted across her face and melted at her side. "Susan, is everything alright?"

She sat straight up and looked down at him. Even before she'd awoken him she'd watched his breathing, slow and steady despite the heart problem. She watched his face, the way he smiled even in his sleep.

Henry's eyes opened. "Susan?"

"Henry, I'm sorry. I'm having a difficult time sleeping."

He raised himself on his arm and sat up. He took her hands. "What is it?"

A warm breeze swept through her skin.

"I had this weird dream," she said. "I'm sorry, but dreams in the past have really meant something."

Henry sat up straighter. Her hands released, he looked into her eyes. "Tell me."

"I was cooking eggs," she said. "Sunny side-up."

"Sunny side," Henry smiled.

"Now stay with me." Susan took a deep breath. "I was cooking these eggs and it suddenly occurred to me the loco moco you love has the same sort of eggs in it. And then I thought of all the loco moco people we've met since I decided to vacation on the islands and it made me think of Rose and all the rest of them, but mainly Rose."

"Why Rose?"

"She was the weirdest. Sorry, Rose," she added, looking up.

"Even weirder than Maverick?"

"Weirder. Okay, so Maverick took you from the hospital grounds and kept you hidden underneath a bed with taped sheets across it to serve as a mattress...but Rose. She dressed up, she had five men convinced she was an old woman. Only on her sixth man did she mess up. He must have guessed who she was."

"Naturally."

"But something about this scenario doesn't add up. How could Rose have kept five old men guessing for months before she took their money? Imagine, getting married to a young woman, thinking it was an old woman. Thinking it was your wife. Unless it wasn't your wife."

"What are you saying?"

"Sunny side-up eggs are like that. Unlike scrambled, they show themselves like clear glass. You can tell where the yolk is, where the white is..."

"Susan..."

"Here me out. I have lately wondered how a young woman could keep an old man guessing, you know. She has to shower sometime. And sleep. And you know, that other part."

"Sex?" He blushed.

"Yeah, that part."

"Well, she must have been good at what she did."

"Yeah, better than you might expect of an old woman." She blushed.

He followed. "So what are you saying?"

"What if Rose is dead but the real Mrs. McLean is still alive?"

"You mean, Sylvia?"

"Yeah. Suppose they worked together, hand in hand. That would keep the old men happy with their wife, never guessing she posed as a young woman when occasion warranted."

Henry laughed and took her by the hand. His face was as red as beet preserves and she could tell he was trying to calm himself down.

"So where is the old woman now?" he asked. "Still aboard ship?"

Now Susan was getting excited. "No. The real Mrs. McLean left the ship along with her husband. And Rose, she was getting close to the jewel fiasco, so close she was killed. I still am not sure by whom. But let's just say she discovered the truth and the truth killed her. So she's dead."

"So, which one snuck downstairs to visit her "beloved" soon after his death? Was it the old Mrs. McLean or the young one?"

"I have a suspicion it was the old one."

Now Henry's eyes were serious. He'd already snapped on the light and his blue eyes were penetrating her own.

"Remember that phone call Jacob got? The one asking him to meet Mrs. McLean at the Cafe' Spritz?"

Henry nodded.

"Mrs. McLean, the old one who'd left the ship earlier with her dead husband, she called Jacob the moment Rose was seen being loaded off the ship.

*　*　*

The following cruise Susan and Henry stayed ashore. There were too many secrets still left uncovered, and no sign of Maverick. When Maverick wasn't to be found, they returned to Jacob.

He actually seemed happy to see them.

"So, been keeping yourself occupied?" Susan asked. The large room smelled stale, sort of like a locker room, but it appeared clean. It was noisy, as usual. Jacob leaned across the table.

"They still think I'm guilty," he said.

"I know, but not for long," said Henry. He leaned in closer. He was sitting next to Susan across the table from Jacob.

"Look. If we can get your help, a lighter sentence for you..."

"What kind of lighter sentence?"

"Let's just say you won't be going to prison for murder."

"So you think I'm innocent? Well, you've got that right." The boy smiled.

"We know you were a part of a jewelry heist," Susan offered. Jacob jumped. "Yeah, so?"

"So..." he turned to Susan, his blue eyes blinking, and then back to Jacob. "So, who would want to kill Rose?"

"Someone who'd discovered what she did for a living, I guess. Or someone who wanted her to keep quiet about something."

"Exactly," Henry said.

"I didn't kill her to keep her silent about the jewelry stuff," Jacob offered.

"Oh, really?"

"I would never kill Rose."

"So what would you like us to know?"

Henry was silent, but the reply was slow.

"Look. Me, Maverick and Candace were all trying to earn a few extra bucks. When Rose found out, she wanted a part of the action, and so we let her have it. Candace was already smuggling in booze to help us do the job. It was pretty scary. We thought Rose could help us because she was so good at dress-up. But one night, Rose didn't meet up with us. I went to the cabin to find out what was keeping her and found her dead. We had no idea who had done it but decided to keep quiet, except for telling you of course." He looked at Susan. "None of us wanted to go to jail."

"Did you tell Maverick to take Henry from the hospital?" She wasn't sure, but Susan felt as if she'd always known Jacob had been the mastermind behind the abduction. It was like him to keep his hands clean, to give the job to someone else. Especially being behind bars, getting Maverick to do it for him would be a fairly easy feat especially if the boy knew their secret was close to being found out.

Henry pulled back.

"It was me, but I did it for your own good. Besides," he smiled, his teeth like pearls, "it was either under the bed or dead on top of it. You guys are looking for a murderer, but she's not on board." He paused, looked around, and continued: "Do you promise, at least for now, to keep what I have to tell you, between us and the... jail?"

"Why?" Henry asked.

"I need you to keep quiet. What I have to tell you will make your hair curl."

"Tell us," Susan insisted, thinking of George who used the same phrase. Perhaps, even in this small way, Jacob had taken something good from his math tutor after all.

"Connections. The murders of both Joe McLean and Rose Anderson, it's all about connections. Listen. While my friends and I were stealing jewels from the pricier homes on the islands and selling the jewels for cash, we discovered what Rose was doing – but we weren't the only ones. Someone else didn't like what she was doing and must have wanted a part of the action. She was always taking extra booze from our place; lots of it, and we wondered why, especially since she was rarely drunk; she didn't like liquor. But the first day when I saw her with the new old guy, I watched them – closely. That old coot was getting booze by the barrelfuls."

Susan thought of the wine stain on the outside deck chair when she'd arrived the first time on the *Aloha*. She thought about the glass, dropped from Joe McLean's hands that first night when she'd met him on deck. Could Mrs. McLean have been drugging him – slowly?

And then she remembered...they'd discovered no poison in that wine glass. No poison within the spill. So what was the answer?

"I heard the conversation between Mr. and Mrs. McLean before he left her and dropped at your feet. Mr. McLean had discovered his wife's identity, and I couldn't believe my ears. When I confronted Rose about it, she denied it at first and then told me she wanted nothing more to do with me. She dropped me like...like a hat."

"What did you do then?" Henry asked.

"And what did she tell you?" Susan countered.

"I left her. The next day when she didn't show up for the group meeting I went back. She was dead. You have to believe me, she was already dead. Did you notice the fish on the side table? I think whoever did it had some way of killing her with the fish. Did you guys ever check that out?"

Susan shrugged. Henry leaned in closer and raised his shoulders. "Yeah, it must have been the fish for Rose but we could never prove it with McLean. Some of the force say McLean ingested amberjack, a tropical fish. But if he did, there's no proven test."

"What about testing the fish?" Susan asked.

"No test for them either. Evidently, ciguatera poisoning is hard to pinpoint; dumbfounds even the doctors. What's important here? Often dehydration accompanies ciguatera, so much so any amount of liquid, wine or anything else, will not curb the thirst. McLean may have had a few episodes like the one on deck before leaving this earth. And maybe the final round was just too much for him."

***

"So we're right about a few things," said Henry. "There must be two murderers. Who had it in for Joe? His wife. But someone else beat her to it. Still, how did they kill Mr. McLean, and why? And Rose? She knew about the jewel thefts. She knew about the booze. And someone had discovered her personal secret."

A sudden thought occurred to Susan. They were back in the hotel room and Susan had just ordered room service. No loco moco, something light; cream cheese on bagels, some orange juice and a bowl of fruit.

"I'm remembering something now Mrs. McLean told me the night I found her crying over her husband. She said something about her granddaughter being angry about what was going on, on the ship..."

Henry's eyes grew large. "You never said anything about a granddaughter," he said.

"I guess I forgot."

Henry wiped his fingers through his red hair. "You don't think..."

"Rose?" Susan queried.

Henry turned pale.

Susan smiled. "Right. The real Mrs. McLean leaves the ship after the death of her husband. Her granddaughter, Rose, is dead. And no one suspects the former..."

"Sure. Life could carry on, and no one would be the wiser, especially if she decided to remain single for awhile. So now what does she do? What would you do?"

"Try to find the murderer of my granddaughter, of course," said Henry.

"Exactly, which makes Jacob's story of hearing from a dead woman by phone, plausible. Mrs. McLean knows she has made a mistake, however. The boy will talk and so she will have to try someone else. Someone who can keep quiet. Well, she can't use the brother, George, he hates her, or a portion of her. She can't use her daughter, Sarah. Or can she? And what about Jacob?"

"Jacob?"

Susan took a bite of the first delivered bagel. It smelled sweet and the texture was soothing. "Look," she chewed, "what was Jacob doing even after he was put in jail? He has tried to help us without incriminating himself; but it's as he said, there are connections all over the place."

"So who are the killers?"

"Quite frankly, I have no idea," Susan said, and took another bite.

The Search Continues

Keith Kealoha and Dorothy Levine knew nothing about the latest antics of Susan and her conspirator, Henry. And they wouldn't. It was Friday, and in another day the *Aloha* would be docking at Honolulu once more.

Susan had made many attempts at soothing the mind of her friend, Jane Dove who was still keeping the *Hotel Camaro* in the black, but Susan figured it was time to give her assistant another raise. This was handled with laughter.

"I wouldn't worry about it. Brianne and Oscar, your favorite neighbors, are hanging on despite the antics of their mother."

"What's been going on?"

"The same. Drinking then thinking she can take care of them. I have taken them under my wing as often as legally possible."

"Thank you for that." Susan pondered on the children who had been with her since the *Scrambled* mystery. Brianne was 9 now and Oscar, 13. He rarely stopped by the hotel anymore, preferring some other crowd, but Brianne, for the most part, was still with them.

"How's Oscar?"

"Pretty rowdy. But I still get him for most meals."

"That's good."

"How's Henry?"

"Fine. I just...oh, Jane, I have no idea when I'll be coming back. Can you possibly hold on for another week?"

"Sure, but what would you think about me hiring an assistant?"

Susan was surprised she hadn't thought of the answer sooner. "Do you have anyone in mind?"

"Actually I do."

"Who is it?"

"Someone from my college days. You've never met her."

"What kind of qualifications does she have?"

Jane laughed. "What sort of qualifications are you looking for?"

Now it was Susan's turn to laugh. All she cared about was the person hired loved kids and was mature enough to handle the responsibilities the hotel demanded. It didn't matter to her if she had a college degree or some certificate from a high school. "Look, I trust you. I'll be home soon anyway."

"Sure." There was a sudden silence on the other end, a silence hard for Susan to interpret.

***

"Where would a woman like Mrs. McLean hide if she couldn't be on board the *Aloha* causing trouble?"

The question provided by Susan made Henry's silence continue. She wondered where Sylvia McLean was, she wondered if George or Sarah would be able to give them further information, and where in the world was Maverick?

"You know, I've been thinking a lot about Maverick these days. There seems to be no trail leading to him; he seems to have just dropped off the planet." Susan was worried. It almost seemed like they were traveling in circles. It was either on land or by sea, but the clues always stopped at key players either dead or missing.

"I have been thinking about Maverick, too. Where would a young man go?"

"Sarah took in Jacob. What about Maverick?"

"She probably doesn't know Maverick."

"But if he's a friend of Jacob's."

"Couldn't hurt."

They traveled back to Sarah's house, but Sarah wasn't home. The place was locked up tighter than a prison, and before long Susan and Henry were traveling over to George's. Maybe he would know something.

140

He was sitting out front on his rickety porch when they drove up. And he wasn't smiling.

"I didn't think you guys would dare to come back," he said, picking at something on his overalls. "The cops have been here."

"What cops?"

"That nasty Kealoha and his partner. And it's funny. They wanted to know if you'd been here. I told them, of course."

Henry smiled. "So, what did they ask?"

"Same such questions as you've been asking. I think they've been trailing you."

Susan turned but she could see no one in the distance.

"Yep, she's a funny one."

"Who?"

"Your partner. Thinks she's a cop."

Susan tried smiling. She tried to keep all of her inadequacies inside and remain focused on the duty at hand.

"So did you know a Maverick Jordan?" Henry asked.

"No."

"He's a friend of Jacob's."

"What's he like?"

"Long hair. Plays the guitar..."

"Funny guy."

"So you know him?"

"No. Just sounds like a funny guy."

A sudden scent of sweat mixed with sour milk met up with Susan's nose. "Been drinking recently?" she asked.

The man stared. "Yep. What makes you ask?"

Susan coughed. "No reason."

"Sorry, but my stash is my stash."

"You have a stash?" she asked.

"You pretend to be so innocent. The other cops asked me the same thing."

"What did they ask you?"

"Look. It was just to protect my boy, Jacob."

"And his friends," Susan added.

"I didn't know about them, only Jacob. He needed the money and I needed the booze."

"You said something a few weeks ago about your brother and some jewels."

"Yeah. He knew all about that."

"About Jacob and those who worked with him," Henry said.

"I guess. You folks sure do ask a lot of questions."

"That's our job," Susan said and then regretted her comment as she watched the old man roll his eyes.

George smiled. "You know," he said finally, "I used to have a way with women. They actually liked my company. My brother, he could never figure it out. Stayed single for at least a hundred years and then glued himself to some woman who is as crazy as a caged bird. All that does is get him killed. But he was a fine ship's captain, and one to notice details, if you know what I mean. Funny, if you ask me."

Henry nodded. "Do you think he knew more than he told you about the jewels?"

"Stuff that would make your hair curl," George said. "Those kids aren't the only ones involved at any rate."

"Why do you think that?" she asked.

"I haven't told you everything."

Susan and Henry waited. The old man scuffed his dirty toe against the wooden deck and played with the fray on his overall shorts. "Look, no trouble, okay? I'm too old to go to jail and far to old to change my ways. Understand?"

They both nodded and watched as the old man stood and turned in the direction the ship would be docked in just one day.

"Joe was a great ship's captain and hadn't seen his friend, Steve, for years."

"Steve?"

"The new ship captain. And quit interrupting me or I'll forget something. Let's see, where was I?"

"You were talking about Steve," Susan said and stopped herself. "Sorry," she added.

"It was funny. His new wife wanted to take a cruise on their honeymoon and my brother found out his old friend, Steve Starling was the ship's captain. He was pretty excited. But when he got on board his friend didn't have time for him. He called to tell me it was disappointing. He also said his own wife had changed, he just couldn't figure it out. One minute she appeared to love him, the next...well, I told him to do some detective work. I told him it just wasn't like someone to love you one moment and deny you the next, whether the person was an old friend or a new wife."

"Joe laughed about that, then told me he'd heard some talk about some jewelry smuggling. I didn't laugh because Joe could always sniff stuff out pretty quick. Said he thought his wife was involved. Thought that was strange because she'd never been on a cruise before. He was going to talk to the captain about it, since they were friends and all. Besides, it was a crime and my brother didn't like crimes."

Susan smiled now and looked over at Henry. She must have given herself away because George was suddenly sitting down and picking at something else on his overalls. "Now, I know what you're thinking," he said. "But I'm the bad blood, Joe was always the good, until he married that woman and she killed him."

"You think so?"

"As far as I'm concerned, that flaky woman got just what she deserved."

***

That night, Susan couldn't sleep. Henry had finally taken another room across the hall. Said it was too difficult otherwise.

Thoughts of she and Henry being together still hadn't managed a reality and Susan wasn't sure what that meant. Were they ever going to be more than friends? Or had the mystery created a division and lack of focus? Perhaps she would never know.

As it was, thoughts of Mrs. McLean, the old Mrs., still running rampant, possibly searching for another husband, kept her from thinking about her own future life. Where would an old woman hide? And what of Maverick? What of the captain on board the ship, *Aloha*? Why would he treat his friend so strangely? Was he caught up in the jewelry smuggling? Or was he just a busy captain with no time for a friend?

Tomorrow, the ship would dock at Honolulu, and then it would head to the other islands for another 6 days of fun in the sun. And she wouldn't be on it. It was funny, but perhaps it just wasn't in her genes to have an entire week on a cruise ship without something bad happening.

Still, there was much left to do. Susan got up and created a list.

1. Talk to Sarah, Rose's mother, one last time.

2. Search for Maverick and Mrs. McLean.

3. See if Candace and Robert will open up even while sweltering in jail.

4. Return to the Kona Movie Theater.

The next morning, tired and cranky, Susan showed Henry the list.

"I can see talking to Sarah or checking at the old theater. But honestly, Susan, the others are too big a fish to even consider at this point."

"But maybe Candace and Robert will talk to us this time." Susan recalled the last talk, especially from the lips of Robert. She doubted, too, they'd get any new information, but didn't they have to try?

"Look, I didn't tell you. We've been banned from the station."

"What?"

"What can I tell you? I have been commanded by my superiors to stop or lose my job."

"But we haven't stopped, we've..."

"Kept going. I know, without involving the Honolulu precinct..."

"And Maverick, Mrs..."

"We haven't had any leads for weeks. A good detective starts at the bottom, uses the leads he has and works his way up. Get it?"

Susan got it and she felt stupid. "I'm sorry," she said.

A warm arm wrapped around her back and held her close. A small tingling reached her arms and entered her heart. It didn't leave.

"I'm sorry. I like your idea of checking out the movie theater again. Let's do that first." They booked the next flight to Kona and within an hour and a half, were once again at the theater. But this had to be the last time, Susan knew that. It was about $200 per person each time they traveled the islands by small plane, and she wasn't sure how long her money would last. Henry helped some, but most of the funds came from her own savings, and her balance was quickly dwindling.

Upon arrival, the man with the bulging red eyes was nowhere in sight.

"What will we do now?" Susan asked.

"Break in."

Susan's heart jumped. Break in? "What if we get caught?"

Henry walked over to the back of the theater. The place was sheltered by old palms and a thousand weeds. "Look. We'll break in through that window." He pointed.

Susan looked at the building. To her right and just a few inches away was a window with half of the dirty glass intact. Henry grabbed a rock. The rest of the glass made a spattering sound as it fell inside the building. Henry took off his shirt. Susan noticed the fine red freckles on his back and tried to keep her mind on the task at hand. Henry took his shirt and placed it on the bottom of the window sill. "Now, climb inside," he said.

Theater Style

Henry grabbed his shirt from the window but didn't put it on. He shook out the glass and tied it around his waist. "I'll look in this room," he said, pointing to the red chairs, although some had fallen over or were nonexistent. Empty holes where chairs should have been were scattered throughout the room. "You look in the other."

A slight chill caressed Susan's arms. "Let's look together," she said.

Henry sighed. "I think we can cover more ground if we're working in different areas."

Susan had a funny feeling inside the theater, almost as if someone was watching them. She imagined the man with the big eyes sneaking around corners with a piece of glass in his hand, the same glass she'd stepped on the moment she'd stumbled to the other side of the window. She didn't want to be alone. "I would feel better if we worked in the same room," she whispered.

Henry nodded. They checked the carpet for clues and jewels, but after a good hour, both came away empty handed. In the old boxes they found nothing but old tickets, programs and other memorabilia that was probably worth something. Susan checked under and near the chairs while Henry scanned the ceiling and walls; she had just reached the last chair when she noticed a previously unseen door.

The old door had a metal knob, but the knob matched the brick colored door in color and because the door also matched the brick walls, its secret had remained a secret...until now.

"Where do you think this leads to?" she asked.

Henry looked up and wiped at his face. "A door? Probably the projector room..."

For a moment Susan thought of the jewels they'd already handed over to the police. Would there be more jewels, or at the very least, a clue to where Maverick or Mrs. McLean could be hiding? "Want to check?" she asked, for another eerie caress had touched her neck, demanding she not go up.

"You go. I'm almost finished here, then I'll join you."

Susan's heart thundered. The prickly sensation made its way up her arms and to her fingers. The door clicked open. Stairs traveled up in front of her. She began the short climb, at least 10 steps, hoping the old wood would hold. Though the old steps creaked and yawned, they weren't dusty and there were no spider webs climbing the walls like in other areas of the theater. It made the climb easier.

At the top of the stairs Susan stopped. Just ahead she could see the movie projector and an empty chair. A window was ahead where the movie would show through onto the screen or stage where she'd just inspected the chairs.

Susan stepped in. The place, though old, was immaculately kept. No dust or cobwebs had accumulated in here either. The room was small and just large enough for a bookshelf, a small table and chair and the movie projector propped up on an old metal stand.

Touching all of these items, Susan's fingers came back dust free. Hearing something, she turned, thinking to see Henry standing there, his hair parted like the entrails of a large fish, but she didn't see Henry.

Her hairs prickled on the back of her neck even before she saw her.

"So you've found me out," the woman said, her painted red lips curving down in hate. She wasn't wearing the sparkling gold dress with the matching shoes and her hair wasn't coiffed or lifted above her shoulders in elegance. She wore plain blue slacks and a matching shirt. Except the shirt and the pants were dirty, and Susan could see more than one smudge on her wrinkled face.

"I...oh..."

"At a loss for words, I can see that," said Mrs. McLean. "But where else was I supposed to live after the murder of my dear husband?"

"Dear? Dear!" The words spilled from Susan's mouth before she could stop them. "You killed your own husband and then left the ship to escape the authorities!"

"I did no such thing!"

"Oh, I'm sure of it." Susan's hands were shaking, as was her legs, but she had to know the truth."

"Sure, I was trying to kill my husband, but...someone thought they needed him dead, first."

"And who was that, pray?"

"Pray? What a funny word."

"So?"

"I didn't kill him, you hear? Sure, I was slowly...killing him, to get the cash, but someone beat me to it." She smiled this time and reached for Susan, who backed away and blocked herself with the chair. She felt like she'd suddenly been caged with a lion.

"He was so angry with me when he found out about the jewels. So angry. But he didn't know everything."

"You mean about your double identity? That you were using your granddaughter, Rose, to help you with your scheme?"

"Keep Rose out of this! Whoever killed her will die!" The woman's claw-like hands reached for her again. Susan dropped the chair; it clanked to the floor, its legs in the air. She traveled to the bookcase and lifted an old movie, still on its reel, holding it before her.

"That reel won't keep you safe," the old woman spat, walking closer, her shoes scratching against the wood floor. She reached for the reel. Susan's heart pounded.

"Do you know you're a pretty good detective for never having been one?" she said. "My husband, dear man that he was, was pretty observant too. After we entered the ship and Rose took my place for a time, he was quick to observe I wasn't the same woman. But he'd already been poisoned enough before coming on board. I expected him to die within a couple of weeks. Other men had met their deaths at about that time. I just didn't think to be found out so soon. His eyes were bad after all."

The words Susan wanted to say now caught in her throat, but a question remained: How could the old woman have been poisoning her husband? Nothing was found in the wine glass, nothing was discovered within the spill on deck... Perhaps now she would know the complete truth. If not the amberjack fish then...

"You think I'm crazy, and maybe I am, but there's not a lot a woman of my age can do to earn a living."

For a brief second Susan thought of her friend, Martha Boaz, now dead. But only for a moment.

"So if you didn't kill your husband, who did?" she asked.

"I have no idea. He wasn't worth much; something I'm just beginning to find out. All of his relatives are in the same boat, so to speak. If it wasn't for the fact I could earn some real money on jewels the entire marriage would have been a mistake."

"So where did you get the jewels?" Susan asked.

Mrs. McLean smiled for the first time. Suddenly Susan realized how little her last name fit her personality or habits. She probably hadn't had a bath in days.

"Actually, that was Rose's doing. She had the energy for that sort of thing. All I know is she left the ship and returned with the goods. We'd split them up between the six of us."

"So George, he was a part of it, too?"

"George? I heard he was some old and crazy coot. No. There was Rose and myself, and Maverick, of course, and Candace and Robert."

"But that's five."

"I know that." Mrs. McLean smiled. Her voice was low and almost imperceptible. "I wasn't clear on who the other person was. That's why I came here, to find out for myself. But all I found was dust, boxes, and a little room I could hide in until I found out where the jewels had been hidden."

"Does the old man know you're here?"

"You mean the man with the bad breath and wandering eyes? No. Why should he?"

"How long have you been here?"

"Just since leaving the ship with my dear husband. But I couldn't stay with him long, they would have questioned me..." She paused. "Sarah kicked me out. She blamed me for her daughter's death."

Mrs. McLean was still just inches away and it was all Susan could do to stand still. The woman appeared to have no weapon and yet she had killed men with less.

"So what will I do with you?" she asked.

"Me?" Susan tried to breathe without choking. The woman couldn't know she was afraid. And where in the heck was Henry?

"No one must know where I am." Mrs. McLean walked a few steps to the bookshelf. Reaching up to the highest shelf, she pulled down some thick gloves. They squeaked as the plastic encased her hands. She reached again to the shelf and retrieved a small, clear vial.

"I no longer have the mask," she said. "These will have to do."

She opened the small lid carefully.

"So what do you think? Do you want to take it straight or with a little wine?"

Susan jumped, and with a strength she didn't know she had, hurled her body towards the door, pushing the old woman into the wall as she fled down the stairs. A slight thump entered her ears but she didn't look back. Clump, clump, clump. She was nearing the bottom when she saw him.

"Henry!"

"What is it?" he asked.

SUNNY SIDE-UP

Opportunity

"Stop!"

The vial crashed to the ground, sending liquid up the bookcase.

Henry raced in and Susan followed him up. At the top of the stairs Henry was holding Mrs. McLean, fast.

"So, looks like you made it from underneath the bed," the woman laughed.

Henry smiled. Susan watched as his eyes sparkled. He clasped the old woman's wrists in hand cuffs. "This will have to do for your jewelry now," he said. "Shall we go?"

Susan could smell a slightly sweet smell wafting through the room, but she didn't reach for the vial. The gloves the old woman had haphazardly discarded, and prompted by the comment of the mask that the woman said she didn't have, told her all she needed to know.

"This is just what we need to convict her," Susan said, looking down at the poison surrounding the shattered glass, and then at Mrs. McLean.

Mrs. McLean didn't look at her. "Anything for my darling Rose," she said.

***

Keith Kealoha and Dorothy Levine stood agape; that was the best way to describe it in Susan's eyes. Following Sylvia's lockup, they asked questions like there would be no end to them. In the end, Susan left the precinct with Henry, happier than she'd ever been.

Finally, the investigation was looking up. Mrs. McLean was caught, a stash of diamonds and other jewels had been located inside an old chair at the theater, (found by Henry while she'd been upstairs with Sylvia) and Candace and Robert would remain behind bars. What these new developments meant for Jacob Carlson was another story.

"So, do you still think Jacob was involved?"

"Of course. But I'm not convinced he was involved with just the jewels. He may have had a reason to kill both Mr. McLean and Rose."

"And what reason would that be?"

Henry brushed his fingers through his red hair. "Perhaps he wanted it all."

"You mean the money from Mr. McLean as well as the money from the jewels?"

"Exactly. Let's imagine once he'd confronted Rose about her indiscretions in jewel theft, she counted him in, but when Jacob also wanted part of the money Rose had gathered from her dead husbands', perhaps Rose drew the line."

"And so Jacob killed her?"

"Maybe. What do you think?"

"I'm not sure."

Henry took her by the waist. "Perhaps you're right, but that leaves Joe's brother, George, and Sarah, Rose's mother. Or Candace or..."

A sudden thought occurred to Susan. "What about the captain and the ship's medical officer?"

Henry looked at her with glittering eyes. "What motive would either of them have?"

"Let's take the captain. He knows Joe McLean personally, right? Joe comes on board to get married and to renew his friendship with the captain. But in renewing this friendship, he discovers something about his own wife that worries him. For one, his wife is different, changed somehow. He asks for help." The question returned to Susan's mind; she could no longer ignore it, and so she added: "Mrs. McLean told me up in *that* room she was slowly poisoning her husband. With what? There was no poison in the wineglass and no poison in the spill. No poison in her husband's body, though he had some weird signs like rashes and dehydration that couldn't be missed. Can you extricate poison from amberjack fish?"

Henry shook his head. "I have no idea, and it will be some time before we get the word from forensic." He reached for her, but she wasn't finished yet. She held up her hand. "Let's suppose she was slowly killing her new husband, dragging the months out before he died so she could get the most money... and in the interim her husband finds out what she's been doing... he finds out there are two Mrs. McLean's and that he's been duped."

"But what of the jewels?" asked Henry.

"Mr. McLean, Joe, could have found out about them, too," Susan said, her mind whirling. "This was a crime the captain would have to know about along with the double identity switch. Joe McLean had to have told Captain Starling what was happening on board with his wife!"

***

Henry had been excited to hear a full report concerning the poison Mrs. McLean had used to murder her husband, and Susan had been delighted.

"You mean she was poisoning him with the "dime" stuff?"

"Dimethylmercury."

"Yeah, that."

"Seems there was plenty of opportunity on board ship."

"So no wine?"

"Too obvious, perhaps. The drug does some wonderful things, though, to your hearing and speech. Let's just say you have a difficult time doing much of anything."

Susan thought about Mr. McLean then; thought about his drunken state that, after all, had probably had little to do with alcohol...and perhaps nothing to do with amberjack fish...

"Did the police find the same drug on the amberjack next to Rose's body?"

Henry blinked. "The police wondered about that, too. With the help of forensic, they've been delving deeper into the mystery..."

***

Though it was a challenge to get back on the ship, *Aloha*, for the first time, Susan and Henry had the support of the Honolulu Police Department. Sure, it was the fourth week since Susan had started this madness, but maybe, finally, everything would pan out and she could leave the cruise ship and all it hadn't offered her, for good.

The new black wig on Susan's head was itchy. Besides the fact that she was dressed like a tourist with one of those flower tops, she also wore dangly palm tree earrings and flamingo shoes in bright pink that matched her shorts.

Henry was dressed similarly, but in a long, blond wig. His T-shirt was aqua green, and he had on khaki shorts and black flip flops. He was smiling down at her.

"Boy, you look hot," he said.

Susan blushed. "You look pretty good yourself," she said, pulling at his wig. "Like some sort of hippie."

"That's right, laugh at my attire just after I've complimented you on yours."

Susan had taken the name of Jenny and Henry; John, befitting the situation. They stepped on board, just as they had previously done. But this time they were both incognito. And this time they would catch the murderer.

***

Though the captain was saying hello to all of the passengers, she and Henry had not received a hello or a handshake, and this worried Susan. Henry seemed nonplussed and followed her to their cabin. They'd taken an outer deck on the starboard side of the ship and the place was decorated in the usual fare.

Two striped pillows sat at the end of the bed and two mints were already on the pillows. But she wouldn't be staying here and had booked a connecting room. It would be easier to focus on finding the killer if they each had separate rooms.

Henry placed his suitcase on the end of the bed. "I have high hopes one day we'll be sharing a room." It was almost as if he'd read her thoughts and was rethinking their decision. This time he didn't blush but looked at her steadily, waiting for an answer.

Susan looked up at him, and though her heart beat wildly she tried to remain calm. "I think," she said, "I'd better get my bag into my own room."

This time Henry blushed and offered to take her suitcase. They'd purchased some new clothes and necessities at a local clothing shop, trying to keep to their new persona, but frankly, Susan hated to buy clothing she'd never be wearing again. Still, what if it meant they'd finally solve this mystery together and could go back to their regular lives?

Whatever that meant.

Susan had a sickening suspicion their lives would never be the same. They'd grown too close and had shared too much. And yet, the idea of going back home and returning to her job made her heart feel calm. She would be with Brianne and Oscar again, and her friend, Jane would fill her in on all of the details she had missed.

Life would return to normal.

She wondered about Henry in that moment; wondered if he'd return with her totally and completely, or if, yet again, they'd find a reason to remain friends. But her thoughts stopped as Henry pushed the door open to her cabin and sat her suitcase at the end of the bed.

"So, it's another trip," he said. "Maybe after we get this murder investigation handled we can take a real one."

"Maybe." Her heart pounded.

"Come on by in an hour. We'll have some lunch."

Life between them seemed suddenly formal, and for a moment Susan wished this trip was something entirely different than it was. She'd thought never to marry again, but now, as she opened the door to the outside elements, she thought of Henry, breathed in deeply and sighed. In a few hours they would be leaving Honolulu; the ship would leave the shore, and, once again, they would be unlinked from the presence of earth and sand.

***

"Jenny, are you there?"

For a moment she thought she must be dreaming, held in the past when her Henry, then John Middleton, had first spoken to her about the bowl of sugar he'd wanted to borrow. And then she was awake. Fully.

The knocking was incessant. She'd fallen asleep.

She raced to the door. Unlocking it she peered outside. "I'm sorry," she said, embarrassed. "I guess I fell asleep."

Henry was standing before her. He appeared afraid. His wig was a disheveled mess.

"What is it?" she asked.

He pushed himself inside. "Shut the door," he commanded.

"What?" She asked, looking into his blue eyes. "What's happened?"

"You'll never believe it!" he said, grabbing her hand and walking her to the bed. "Sit down."

Susan looked at Henry. His hands were shaking.

"What!?" she asked again, sorry to ask it, but more curious than ever to know what was going on.

"Maverick. He's on board."

"You're kidding!"

"Why would I kid about Maverick? I followed him to his quarters. He's got the same one. The guy has cut his hair short almost to the scalp, and he's changed it to a muted brown, but it's him, I know it."

Susan felt sick. "So what do we do now?"

"Watch him like a hawk. Maybe he's the murderer. Or maybe he will lead us to the killer. Perhaps he was on land for awhile and just returned to the cruise ship, hoping the search had blown over."

"Did he see you?"

"Maybe. I'll radio the police station, tell him we've found Maverick. At least they'll know to stop the search on land. Ready for lunch?"

"I thought you'd already eaten."

"Yeah, but I'm still hungry. Besides, we've got to come up with a plan."

Jewelry Thief

After lunch, the two wandered to Maverick's cabin. They couldn't hear him on the other side of the door playing his guitar but they didn't knock. Instead, they followed the long hallway to the pool.

Susan was wearing a one-piece red and yellow suit, and Henry was complementing her with a bright ensemble of his own. The pool reeked of vacationers taking in the full brunt of an island vacation. Neither dared dive in but sat in the lounge chairs surrounding the pool. They listened as an Acapulco band played in the corner and waiters dressed in white shirts and khaki shorts asked for drink orders.

When a waiter walked over for an order she and Henry declined. The waiter walked away but not before Susan noticed Maverick in the distance. He wasn't wearing a suit but was carrying his guitar. It was funny to see him without the hair.

She laughed behind her hand. "You know what? It's almost like you took the kid's hair and now he has yours."

Henry stared at her. "My hair's red," he said.

"Yeah, but I wonder if he's cut and dyed it or if he was wearing a wig before and just took it off."

"Why would he do that?"

"To keep fans away?"

"Does he have fans?"

"Who knows. Look, he's talking to someone."

"That's Charles, the chief medical officer."

"Sure looks like him."

"I wonder what they're talking about."

She and Henry moved closer. The yelling of those in the pool was covering up anything that might have been overheard just a few feet away...

"You know there's no way..." Charles began.

"Why?"

"The rules are stiff on this ship."

"But I need it."

"Like a hole in the head."

The boy stiffened. "Look, I already told you, it went missing."

"So what am I supposed to do?"

"Supply me. I will help you."

The medical officer looked away and into Susan's eyes. She was staring when she might have been listening. "Need some assistance?" he asked, his small, brown eyes piercing her own.

Susan looked away. "Sorry," she offered.

The two moved away. "Do you think they recognized me?" she asked.

"I'm not sure. Still, one thing's for sure. Maverick knew about the alcohol stored in Rose's cabin."

"He also knew about the jewels. I think they were talking about the supply that went missing; the jewels now at the station when we took Mrs. McLean into custody. And the jewels you found, we can't forget about that..."

"The boys on shore, they say Mrs. McLean isn't talking."

Susan thought of the woman's easy way of speaking inside the theater and was glad for the frightening event. If the poison hadn't been sheltered within the bookshelf as a way of killing Susan after confessing, Sylvia McLean might never have unveiled her little secret, and they'd still be that much further from discovering the truth.

***

Susan struggled to awake; the noise below deck was deafening.

"Henry!" she called.

But the room was dark. She climbed from the bed, reached for the light and surveyed the room. She was alone. With another click she was out the door, her stateroom locked behind her. She knocked on Henry's door. "Ah...John?"

He was at the door. "What? What is it?" He ushered her in. He wasn't wearing his wig. He'd been asleep too and was still in his pajamas – some fabricated silk. They were red and made his hair look orange.

He touched her on the arm and then directed her to sit.

"Who was the guy working with Candace and Robert? You know the one she said kept peering eyes away from what we were doing? You know, the camera guy?" Susan asked.

"The police talked to the man. He no longer works on board. No connection so far other than being paid off with liquor to force the camera down the wrong hall. But he may know something about the killer. They're still questioning him."

"Why didn't you tell me?"

Henry brushed his fingers through his hair. "I guess I figured it no longer mattered. Sorry."

"That's okay," Susan offered. "I just wanted to check that we'd thought of everyone in this murder fiasco, that's all." She thought of the dream, the loud noise she thought she'd heard below deck, and decided to brush it aside. In her dream, she'd been crawling down there, searching for something...

He smiled, reached over and took her hand. "I've been thinking," he said, "after this is all over maybe you'll reconsider my proposal."

She sat still. The conversation had changed and she didn't like it.

"I mean, what would be so bad about getting married? Imagine the fun we'd have finding all kinds of murderers."

"What do you mean?"

"You know, seeking out the bad guys, together?"

Susan tried to swallow. "I'd like to avoid searching out murderers ever again."

"But I thought..."

"You thought wrong." She stood, releasing his hand. "Marriage is a big decision...I..."

"I know." He colored then and turned to face the window. "I mean, we're right for each other."

"Except for one thing."

Henry turned toward her and it was all she could do to lie to him now. "Love...what about love?" she asked.

But she'd said the wrong words.

"So you do love me!"

"Yes, but..."

"Look, I know I'm no perfect guy. I have this heart condition. I may no longer have a job with the department if things fizzle here, and even if they do work out... But I love you, you've got to know that." He was at her side, leaning in to her. "Please, Susan. You have to know how much I care..."

Susan couldn't help it. She caressed his hair and worked her fingers over his face. "I care about you too, but..."

"You're afraid, I get that. You want your second marriage to be a far-cry different adventure than your first." He touched her face. "You see, Susan, we are meant to be together."

It was one of the oldest lines in the book but the words still touched her. "How do I know you will always be with me, really *with me*?" she asked, a large lump sliding up her throat. "What if it's all about you. What if you decide your love isn't as strong as you thought or I'm too much of a klutz for you or something?"

"A klutz?" His hand was now caressing her neck. "What are you talking about?"

"You know how I mess up investigations, say things that are better kept silent. I have no idea how to find a real criminal."

"But I thought you didn't care about that." He laughed. "Susan. I thought we were going to give that up."

"You'd really give it up?"

"I was only joking before... sure."

She could feel his breath on her face. The smell of his hair and aftershave. And when he looked at her she could see love there. Did her own eyes say the same? She was shaking now, but it wasn't from fear. And he was looking at her, really looking at her, and there was no question what was going to happen next.

The touch of his lips was soft at first, and when his kisses became more insistent her arms couldn't help but wrap around him taking him in, again and again...

***

A kiss. He'd asked for nothing more, but the way he would forever look at her from then on had changed and in a strange but powerful way they began to work better together.

It started the following day when the ship docked at Maui. They'd gone to see Charles. He was sitting at his desk in the infirmary going over some papers. No one else was in the room and it occurred to Susan there was little reason for others to be there. Rose was dead and the old Mrs. Sylvia McLean was behind bars.

The medical officer looked up. He didn't appear to know them, but his forehead was creased with his own questions. "Feeling sick?" he asked.

"Why, yes. My...wife here, she's been feeling sick since the fish last night."

"Fish?" the man asked, leading her to the table and directing her to sit down.

"Yes," Susan mumbled, hoping she'd changed her tone enough. Though her disguise was intact she couldn't be sure her voice would hold true.

"Let's have a look." The ship's officer pressed on her belly. "Does this hurt?" he asked.

"Yes," she lied. "What's wrong?"

"There was an epidemic on one of our previous cruises."

"What happened?"

The man blinked in Henry's direction. "Well, there's always a chance of ingesting bad fish in one of the local seafood restaurants. Did you order any tropical fish?"

Susan nodded her head.

"We don't serve it here on board. Too dangerous. So you must have gotten it offshore."

The man looked at her, his eyebrows raised. "Have you had diarrhea, dizziness, a rash...anything like that?"

"No," Susan lied, though she hadn't had any of the above symptoms.

"What's your name?"

"Su...I mean Jenny. I ah...why do you have to know that anyway?"

"Have you been feeling anxious or confused?"

Susan thought about that. Well, she had felt both anxious and confused, but neither symptom had anything to do with eating fish.

"Didn't you say people on board had gotten sick because of some fish?" she asked.

"Yes." He hesitated briefly. "Seems like folks like to complain about the inadequacy of the ship's food, but quite often they eat fish off shore. How about a strange cold/hot sensation?"

"Like what?" Susan asked.

"When you touch an object in a room the object tricks you into thinking it's cold to the touch when it isn't and warm to the touch when it's cold."

"That's strange," said Henry.

"It should be," said the doctor. "Well?"

"I haven't felt anything strange like that," said Susan.

The man's steely brown eyes lit up for an instant. "You should be fine. If the pain gets worse or you experience any vomiting or diarrhea, or anything else I've mentioned, come back and I'll check you further."

"How long does it take for a person to die from the poisoning you're speaking of?" Susan asked.

"Ciguatera?" The man raised his bushy eyebrows.

"Just curious," Susan offered.

"One doesn't usually die, that is, if they're healthy and get treated at a hospital quickly. That is to say, if the doctor knows the signs of such a poisoning..."

"It reminds me of the old man who died on board," Susan began. "I think his name was McLean."

The doctor was silent.

"You remember him?"

Henry nudged her. She was now off the table and standing by his side. But suddenly, she felt sick... remembering she was just putting on an act, she tried to slow her breathing.

The doctor patted her on the back. "Listen, just come back if you start feeling worse. As far as I know you have ship nausea, a common ailment on cruise ships."

"Of course." Susan shook his hand. It was rough and reminded Susan of sandpaper. They left the room and walked up the hall. But Henry was laughing.

"I thought he almost croaked on the spot when you asked him about Mr. McLean. Didn't you notice how white his face went?"

Susan shook her head.

"Look, if you're going to be a good detective, you've got to observe what is going on around you. Besides the fact the man went pale, I noticed his right hand shaking."

"All I saw was I was beginning to feel sick just talking about me being sick."

Henry took her hand. It was warm and smooth and unlike the chief medical officer's. "Do you think," she said, stopping Henry for a moment and looking into his eyes, "the medical officer lifts weights or something? His hands weren't smooth like I expected. It was almost like he worked in the forests on his free time chopping wood or something."

"Are you serious? I mean, a ship's doctor would never have time for lumber work. He wouldn't have time on land to do much of anything, being on the ship all of the time."

"That's what I thought, too. But what else could his rough hands mean? Did you hear anyone else besides Maverick in the room when they had you under that bed? Perhaps Maverick wasn't the only person involved."

"Well, we already know that," said Henry, still holding her hand and looking into her eyes.

Susan thought of all those involved. Mrs. McLean, Rose, Jacob, Candace and Robert, but none of them were large enough in stature to kidnap someone without a stronger accomplice. One who might know the islands, one who was older and could be in charge. Sure, Maverick might have taken Henry from the hospital, but what if someone else had planned it, someone who could keep everyone in line while on the ship.

"So, who did you hear in the room?" Susan asked again.

"Well, I'm pretty sure the person was Maverick," said Henry, "but now that you mention it, I heard other voices. But they could have been those we have already questioned."

"Except we haven't questioned Maverick. Maybe it's time to talk to him."

***

Maverick was walking past the *Raspberry Deck* when Susan saw him. It was another new morning, they were still in Maui, and she was hoping today would be the day the can of worms would

165

open up. She was wearing the black wig and an outfit fit for a tourist queen.

He looked up. "Hi," he said.

"Hi." She looked down at him. "Are you the guitar player?"

He appeared to squirm.

"Maybe. Have we met?"

She lowered her voice. "No," she said. "I just love guitar players," she said.

"Really? How old are you?" he asked.

Henry had made her up to look younger than she was but the boy had seen through the disguise – maybe too far through. "Ah, 25."

The boy coughed. Fortunately, Henry was listening just a few feet away, at the corner of the opposite corridor. If the next few moments got scary he'd promised he would come to her aid. She counted on that more than she'd let on.

He grinned over at her. "So, you think I'm that guitar player. And I think you're a bit older than you're letting on."

Susan's heart pounded.

He stared at her.

"Did you know Rose?"

"Everyone knew Rose. She was quite the gal. How did *you* know her?"

Susan gulped. "Well, um, I saw her in a couple of shows. She was good."

"Must have been a past show," Maverick said. "How many cruises have you been on?"

"Quite a few," Susan said truthfully.

"Well then, you must also know I was pretty close to her. If you're thinking I'm ready to date..."

"Oh, no, no, I just wanted to talk to you, that's all."

"And get my number, is that it?"

Susan would have laughed if he hadn't looked so serious. "I just need you to answer some questions for me," she said.

"Like what?"

"Well, like if Rose was a drinker."

The boy stood straighter. "She drank a little. So what?"

"Just asking."

"Are you the police?"

"No."

"Then why would you care what Rose drank?"

"I...ah..."

"Listen, lady. I'm never going to date you no matter how close you try to get to me by trying to understand my girlfriend. She was the best thing that ever happened to me...through everything. Now I have to go. And try to pick up guys your own age, will ya?"

Susan watched Maverick leave down the opposite hallway. Henry waylaid him. She didn't know what he said, but the boy walked away even angrier than when she'd spoken to him.

***

"You did fine," Henry told her. "He thought you were a real kook."

"So. We haven't learned anything new."

"False." They were walking up the hall to she and Henry's rooms. "He admits Rose was his girlfriend. When I stopped him I told him I knew about the booze and the jewels and about the murder of Rose. I asked him if he did it."

Susan was flabbergasted. "Do you want to get us killed?"

"I told him he'd better be careful. People were talking and he'd be found out."

"So why open the can of worms, so to speak?"

"To get him to move. You were too nice."

"Too nice! He thought I was trying to pick him up."

"Exactly," said Henry.

***

That night they followed Maverick. It was right after his performance; his first of two on the ship. The second would be performed on Wednesday as they'd previously discovered. He still had the blond wig on. His performance must have been poor; he was fuming.

At the captain's door, Maverick knocked and went inside.

SUNNY SIDE-UP

Surprising Revelation

"Holy cow!" said Henry.

"How are we going to hear anything now?"

Henry turned the corner with Susan in tow. Leaning in, he said: "Look, there's something fishy going on here and it may just have to do with the captain."

"Duh."

Henry took Susan in his arms and kissed her. The kiss was quick and sweet but her heart pounded like a hundred she-goats. He touched her hair.

"Look, we've got to get in there, somehow. I want you to go to the kitchen. Put on something kitchen-y, grab some food and put it on a plate and come back here in your garb. Then I want you to knock on the door."

"That hardly seems fair. I'll guard the door; you can go and get the stuff. I think it's better if you go in."

"Really Susan."

"Should I put my life at stake in there? Nope, and neither should you. Unless you want to grab a cup and listen at the door."

Henry laughed.

"I mean it. I've heard it works."

"With all of the people walking by, I'm afraid not. It may be the only way to hear, but I'm far from ready to take a chance being seen by the cameras or..."

As if on cue, people walked passed them in evening attire.

"Both of us ought to be safe. What if the captain has a gun in there, or poison?" Susan asked.

"You're probably right." He took her hand.

"Let's wait it out; follow Maverick when he comes out.

***

According to Susan's watch, Maverick had spent 25 minutes in the captain's quarters. When he left, they followed him and watched as he traveled back to his room and shut the door.

Moments later he was down the hall again, and leading them to the door that led to the freezer hold. Susan knew they were probably being watched but she couldn't worry about that, she had other worries.

Susan's arms chilled when Maverick entered the freezer compartment and shut the door. Once inside, she and Henry waited for his return. They slid inside another compartment and waited for Maverick to pass.

A few minutes later, they were following Maverick up the steps to the lower deck. He had something in his hands. It smelled like fish.

Following the boy to his cabin they watched for re-entry to the hallway, but it grew dark and Maverick still hadn't left his cabin. Near 9 p.m., with guitar in hand and a blond wig on his head, he shut the door to his room and proceeded up the hall.

"So what do you think?" she whispered to Henry.

Henry grew solemn. "Either Maverick ate the amberjack in his room or he's setting them aside for later. Remember Rose's room and the fish at her side? What if Maverick knew the fish was contaminated? What if he needed to kill her to protect his own hide?"

"Then why speak to the captain?"

"I have a funny feeling about the captain," Henry said.

***

An hour later, she and Henry were discussing who Maverick might consider killing to protect his secret. They both decided jewel theft might be enough and booze smuggling was minor in comparison to the former crime. And then there was the kidnapping scenario. What had Maverick wanted to keep Henry from finding out? Was it all of this, or something else that had broken the camel's back?

"What reason would Maverick have to kill Mr. McLean?" she asked.

"That's what bothers me. I can see a motive for killing Rose, but for Joe McLean? Unless Joe really did know about the jewels."

"And he went to the captain about them. I think you're right," said Susan. "I think the captain is the head of it all and he killed Joe McLean."

"His best friend?"

"Well, what would you do if your friend came to you with accusations jewel smuggling was happening on your ship? And what if you were involved? What if..." Susan pointed her finger at Henry and pushed him to the bed. "What if the captain killed Mr. McLean and Rose Anderson to protect his hide? What if all those kids are working for him and he keeps them silent with a little money and a lot of free booze?"

Henry looked up at her. "So," he said, still lying on the bed as she leaned in front of him, "Mrs. McLean and her granddaughter, Rose, get caught in their husband killing scheme. They feel pressured having the captain involved but know their hands are tied. They ask for his silence. In return they will get him the money he wants."

"I thought captains made loads of money," said Susan.

"Oh. Then maybe it isn't the captain." Henry sat up and pulled her to the side of him. Wrapping his arm around her he continued: "Maybe we're missing a piece here. What about the chief medical officer?"

"What about him?"

"What reason would he have to kill Mr. McLean and Rose Anderson?"

***

That night as Susan slept in her cabin with the sliding door to the deck open just ajar enough to let in the moist air, she thought about the chief medical officer and how he might be a part of the whole scheme. She tried to remember every instance in which she'd spoken with him or had learned something new.

171

She'd gone into the chief medical officer's infirmary when she'd feigned sickness. She and Henry had watched him talking to Maverick near the pool. His steely eyes had bored into her whenever she'd asked a question...

If the chief medical officer, Charles, was killing people to cover up something he was doing, how would he do it? For a medical officer, the poisoning would come easy – so Mr. McLean's death might naturally come from someone with medical access. The investigation was getting stranger and stranger the longer Susan thought about it. But as her eyes closed and she drifted off to sleep all she could think about was Henry.

***

"Ah...Henry!" She pounded on Henry's door before she realized her mistake.

The door swung open. "What is it?"

Susan slid inside. "Last night I went over all of the facts concerning the chief medical officer. He obviously had access to poison and I remember Jacob saying something about Charles watching us."

She sat. "Then I started thinking about something else. It made the hairs on the back of my neck stand up. I woke up and looked at the clock; it was close to 3 a.m. All I could think about was who was also on deck that night when Mr. McLean was found dead."

"Charles, the medical officer!"

"That's right." For the first time Susan really looked up at Henry. He was in his silk pajamas once again and his fine red hair was falling in a mismanaged heap.

"Sorry," she said.

"No sorry needed. Let me get a shower and I'll meet you back at your place in half an hour."

Susan stood and walked to the door. "See you then," she said.

Half an hour later she returned, knocked on Henry's door, remembered the appropriate name, and stood waiting for Henry to open his door. But no one came and the door wasn't locked.

Entering, she peeked around the corner. "Henry? I'm here."

172

But there was no answer. She checked in the bathroom. It appeared Henry had had a shower; also his shaver was balancing precariously on the edge of the sink. She turned, looked into Henry's room and studied the place. As a last resort she checked under Henry's bed.

But Henry wasn't there.

***

"Where is he?" Susan yelled.

Maverick was nonplussed. He stood before her, rigidly, as if somehow afraid.

"Where is who?"

"Hen...I mean John."

"John who?"

"Middleton."

"What does he look like?"

"Tall. ah...blond hair. Freckles.."

"Oh, that guy. Your friend. I haven't seen him."

He tried to walk past her but she followed him. She grabbed him by the arm. "Tell me now!"

"I can get security, ma'am," he said.

"That would be good! Then we can put you where you belong."

The boy with the now short hair smiled at her. "And where would that be, ma'am?"

"In jail!"

"Really, lady."

Susan breathed in. She was handling this all wrong. "Look, I'm worried about him. I promise, if you let him go we'll say nothing about the jewels or the...the booze."

"What do you know about that?" Maverick grimaced. He clutched her other arm. Her fingers fell away from him.

"I know you've been stealing jewels and the captain has been keeping you quiet with alcohol. Sure, the booze had to be signed for, but the captain must be good at doing what is necessary."

Steely eyes met her own. "So, you must be... Susan?" the boy asked. "I should have realized. I thought you were just trying to pick me up..." He pushed her in front of him, and still holding her arm, directed her down the hallway.

Nowhere to Go

"Sit here!" Susan looked over at Maverick. He was pulling someone from the closet. *Henry.*

He sat Henry, now wigless, next to her on the bed. Everything appeared intact, including the mattress. Henry appeared drugged; he wouldn't look at her and he smelled almost as sour as before. He had a long multi-colored sash holding his mouth closed.

"What do you want from us?" Susan asked, trying to keep her voice steady, but her hands were shaking.

Hatred met her. "You have no idea what you're doing," Maverick said, releasing the sash from Henry's mouth. "No idea."

Henry blinked. "Maybe you could tell us," he queried.

The boy sat across from them on a desk chair. Wiping his hands on his jeans he said, "How do I keep you guys quiet?"

"Quiet? From whom?" Henry asked.

"You ask too many questions." Maverick appeared to consider his next words and all Susan could think about was Henry had been drugged – again.

"I have to be careful now. But perhaps you can help me."

Susan watched Henry's face but he showed no emotion now. Maybe she should say something, but she didn't know what. The room smelled of death; empty alcohol bottles were stacked in one corner and an all consuming stench of rotten fish permeated the room.

"You live here?" Susan asked, staring at the man who had kidnapped them both.

"Well, what was I to do? Best time for your man here is when he's weak or taking a shower." He laughed. "You should have seen his face when I walked into the room."

"'Susan,' he squeaked. 'Is that you?'"

I almost laughed. I thought, "Here we are in the beginning of a romance and I can be a part of it."

Henry might have slugged him then, but his hands were handcuffed in front of his body in a sort of V, and the feat might have been a bit of a challenge. But she could see the challenge in his eyes. She wondered where the key to the cuffs was.

"So what to do now." Maverick left the chair and paced the untidy and smelly room.

"Maybe you should check with the captain," Susan said.

"The captain? Why would I do that?" He stopped pacing and sat down, the air growing thick around him. "Do you have any idea the trouble I'm in?"

"We can guess," Henry said.

Maverick rubbed his hands against his jeans. "Look, you two have been a problem since the beginning. How does a jewel thief get around with two – I mean one snooping cop around. Susan...Susan, Rose spoke of you highly, even in her last breath."

"You killed her." It was a statement rather than a question.

"What was I supposed to do?" The boy's hands covered his face and Susan wondered if the strong young man was crying. "You know, my life would have been fine, just fine if you two hadn't arrived on board. Rose, she was pretty good at what she did but she could have made even more money if she'd let me join in. But she wanted to tell the police. Can you believe it?"

The boy sniffed and rubbed at his face. For the first time Susan saw him for the young man he was. Early 20s, just starting out in life, fearful of empty pockets. And yet, he was cruel too. He had killed Rose without even a thought.

"I suppose you think I'm a bad person," he said now as if reading her thoughts, "but I'm a decent guy. I loved Rose."

"More than the jewels?" followed Henry.

"A guy has to earn a living," said Maverick, "and it was difficult making a living on board ship. My wage was cut and I was thinking to try another place. But you know how it is...Then, a few months ago I received the offer of a lifetime. Steal the jewels and bring in part of the profit. And then Rose came into my life. Unfortunately, she didn't want to share anything. I got angry."

The boy withdrew his hands from his face and looked at them. "You know about Mrs. McLean then." His face was red and tear stained.

Henry nodded as Susan watched. Perhaps, in this terrible act of abduction something good would come.

"We know there were two women playing the part," said Henry, shifting on the bed, though Susan knew he wouldn't be able to get comfortable with the handcuffs on. She touched him on the arm and then withdrew.

Maverick was grinning over at her. "Who would have thought you'd become a team in more ways than one."

"You killed Rose..." she began.

"I had to. She was going to tell the captain and I couldn't allow that." Maverick paused, wiped his hands on his jeans and looked away. "You know, I should have figured it would turn out like this. After Joe McLean's death my life got scary. I was always running errands for the captain; trying to keep you two from figuring out what was going on. Joe's death was just the beginning of my misery and I guess you want to know who killed him."

"That would be nice," Susan said.

He laughed, but it was more like a sputtering cough. "So would I. At first I thought Rose had done it, decked in old lady attire. She knew about poison, having worked for the chief medical officer before Candace jumped on board. You know the two are sisters."

Henry nodded. "We also know Rose and the real Mrs. McLean are grandmother and granddaughter."

"That too. They had quite the scheme going if you ask me. Unfortunately neither wanted to share in the wealth. Rose would have managed McLean's death, too, if someone else hadn't stepped in. She and her counterpart were killing him slowly, but the time hadn't arrived yet; the plan was to get through the cruise and once at home let the geezer have it for all he was worth. You know what's funny? That old man wasn't worth a cent. I found this out later, after Rose was dead and I wondered when the real Mrs. McLean was going to collect. I searched her out in-between cruises and finally discovered her at the Kona Movie Theater, scrounging for the jewels. I told her I was going to turn her in." He laughed. "You know, she tried to poison me, thinking I was stupid or something. In the end I left her there, dirt and all, and hid the jewels practically in front of her eyes. That old geezer was there, but she didn't want him to know she was there. So she hid mostly, and searched when she could, but I'd hidden the jewels too well for her old eyes."

"Why didn't you just kill her?" Susan asked.

The boy's face grew pale. "I just couldn't, knowing she was Rose's grandmother..."

"*I* found the jewels," Henry said, though Susan wondered why he'd spoken.

The boy breathed heavily and reached for Henry. The blond wig was already removed and as Maverick pulled on the strands, Henry winced.

"So where are they?" Maverick asked.

"At the police station under lock and key."

"Figures," Maverick said, releasing his grip. "Still, when I kill you folks, old as you are, I can get the money promised to me."

"From the captain?" Henry asked.

The boy smiled, his eyes twinkling. "Sure, he'll pay me for killing you, or should I say, having a luxurious meal alone in your stateroom. Should I make it yours, Susan, or should it be in your beau's?"

Susan swallowed, but it was difficult. The amberjack, the boy was going to use the fish as he'd used on Rose Anderson.

***

Susan pulled off the scarf the second Maverick turned from them. "I need to use the bathroom," he said, "but I will have the door open, and you never know who I've got guarding the *other* door." He blinked at Susan and walked to the bathroom.

"Now, you need to listen. When the boy returns, I want you to play along. I want you to play at seduction," whispered Henry.

"What?!"

Henry pointed to the top bunk. "There, on the pillow."

Susan reached for the shiny piece and quickly returned to her place on the bed.

"Se-duc-tion," Henry hissed. "Keep his attention. Do whatever you think will draw him in. And I mean anything."

Susan's heart pounded so hard it hurt. "Okay," she said, her voice barely above a whisper. "But..."

A slight clunk was heard and Maverick entered the room from the bathroom. "I've decided to kill you here," he said. "There will be no escaping. I can always move you later."

The thought of death surrounded Susan like a fog. How could she let it happen... Her mind whirled with ideas, strategies, but there wasn't time to think logically, she just had to do it.

She looked at her captor. "There's something I need to tell you first," she said, making herself captivating by the way she reached for him, and the tone she used – sort of like a woman in need. "You'll want me alive," she breathed. "I could be of real help to you. Besides, I care about you."

Maverick laughed. The sound was long and empty.

"You serious? I told you, you're too old for me."

"Still," said Susan, taking off her wig and brushing her fingers through her brown hair. "I think we could make it work, you and I." She stood, leaving the bed.

"You've got to be kidding," Maverick laughed. "And what, pray, will we do with Henry?"

"Kill him, of course. It's always been you anyway."

"When?"

"When I saw you this morning, that's when I knew."

Sudden shock registered in Maverick's eyes.

"You sound just like Rose," he said. "She was always saying what a couple we made. She was always telling me how it was going to work out between us. She loved me."

He placed the plate of fish on the chair and looked at her. "Rose is that...you?"

"Of course." She tried to laugh, but the laugh was stilted like the forced delivery. She would have to do better.

She walked towards him. "And I can love you, too."

"Rose, do you mean it?"

"I do. Look. I'll stop marrying men for their money and I'll marry you."

Maverick smiled and took her in his arms. "You'd do that?"

The man reeked of alcohol, but Susan remained in the moment.

"Sure. I can let the other men go if I know you'll be a part of my life...forever."

"Oh, Rose...I can hardly believe it. I... " Maverick gasped. But then suddenly he reared back, his last words choking from his pasty lips. With his head back, pulled in the opposite direction from some unknown force, Susan realized Henry had Maverick by the neck with his handcuffs. In an instant, the chair, once holding the precious fish clattered to the floor. Henry pulled Maverick to the door, shouting "Run! Now!"

Susan raced from the room, her wig forgotten. Nothing mattered now except telling someone Henry was in danger.

Trouble

A giant hand reached out and pulled her from her mission. Susan had no idea where it had come from but it was suddenly there, at the end of the hall near the first turn, and when she looked up, the face was unmistakable.

"What are you doing here?" the captain queried, pulling her back up the hallway. She screamed but no one came. "You must be with the slovenly Henry."

"I'm just going to my – room," she stammered. "Let go of me!"

A heavy hand clamped against her lips but it felt strange – like thick rubber. From the corner of her eyes she could see that the captain was wearing a mask, a sort of long shield that covered his face and neck.

He dragged her to Maverick's room. "I can just bet what we'll find in here," he said, opening the door while still maintaining a tight grip.

Henry had Maverick pinned against the wall. The boy was gasping for air.

"I think it's about time you let my pawn go," he said, "or I'll have to kill your little princess."

The captain's hand was still across her mouth, but she was able to kick him in the shin. Released, she ran in the only direction she could. Behind Henry. The door to the room clicked automatically behind them.

She and Henry were trapped.

The captain looked down on them. "So, you think you know it all," he said. He wore his white uniform as always and spoke with emphasis.

Maverick rubbed his neck and sat down on the chair. The fish was still on the floor. Susan avoided it. The smell of the room reeked through her skin; her eyes watered.

The captain turned to Maverick. He appeared to shrink in the chair. "I'm sorry, captain," the young man said.

"Pick up the fish!" the captain yelled.

Maverick scuttled around the room until he'd found them. One was near the closet, the other lay at her feet by the bed. Though Maverick was close he didn't even look at her.

"Now sit and eat!" directed the captain.

The boy looked up; he appeared delirious.

"What?" he stammered.

"Eat!"

"But these..."

"Eat." The sound was firm like a short knock on a door. Susan felt sick. She reached for Henry but he shrugged her away. The handcuffs. They were unlatched.

"So that's how you killed Rose," Henry said, keeping his hands in the same handcuffed position. The captain didn't appear to notice; his *pawn* said nothing.

"Maverick. He has always taken my orders, but he has a funny way of carrying them out." His heavy breathing fogged up the mask.

The captain glared at Henry, and as Susan watched, she noticed Maverick taking the first timid bite. In seconds, the fish was half finished, in another the entire amberjack was down the boy's throat. Had she made a mistake in assuming the boy had killed Rose?

"It wasn't the fish," said the captain.

The boy looked up at the captain. In his eyes were tears. "You mean, I didn't poison Rose?"

"No."

"Then the fish..."

"Oh, this will do the job." He reached for something in his pocket... Grinning, he grabbed the plate of fish. "One is all you're going to need. Besides, I think these folks deserve a taste before I top it off with some added liquid." He opened the vial.

Susan sat up straighter, her breath catching in her throat.

In that moment Henry's fist found the captain's masked face.

Before her next thought, the captain had punched back. A fight ensued, knocking every piece of unbolted furniture to the ground. Susan leapt from the bed. Grabbing the plate that had once again fallen to the floor, she hit the captain on the head, shattering the dish, and reached for Maverick. He'd collapsed on the chair opposite. He opened his eyes widely when she touched him.

"Come! Now!"

She dragged Maverick by the hand and the boy half walked, half ran through the doorway. At the other side she walked him to her stateroom. Pushing him to the bed she re-cuffed him to the side rail. Sure, Henry had been held under the bed a couple of times, but this boy was of a different variety altogether. He was only half there anyway, drugged with alcohol – and poisoned by doctored fish. Would he get sick? Die? She had to do all she could to prevent that.

Racing to the chief medical officer's quarters, she yelled for him at the door. When he came promptly, she was relieved, and he followed her without question to her quarters. He didn't ask why Maverick was handcuffed to the bed, and Susan gave no explanation.

"He's been poisoned! Take care of him!" she yelled before handing him the key and racing back to the room where Henry and the captain were. But they were no longer fighting and Henry was alone.

Henry's lips were bleeding and he was holding his middle. "Get the fish – leave the vial on the ground. We can't be contaminated. Where's Maverick?"

"In my quarters," Susan replied, picking up the last fish with an old towel and carrying it to the bed. "He's with Charles."

Henry turned as white as a sheet. "What?" he asked, standing.

***

At the ship's infirmary, Susan watched as the chief medical officer, Charles, checked Henry's ribs. None were broken, but they were bruised; the cut in his lip superficial. Susan was worried,

183

however. They still didn't know how much Charles was involved but there hadn't been a choice. They'd had to count on him for two reasons. Who knew how the captain had fared.

The man's small brown eyes checked everything, his heavy gray eyebrows twitching. "You'll be fine, " he said, looking at Henry and patting him on the arm. Henry's upper body was swathed with white bandages and his eyes looked tired.

"You did the right thing," he said to Susan.

"I didn't know what to do," she answered, turning to her beloved. "Stay with you. Help you fight some more, or get Maverick to safety."

Someone patted her arm. "Look, now that everything is, shall we say, out in the open, it's time you knew the truth."

"What truth?" she asked.

"It might be a surprise to you," said Charles. "I've been trying to figure this mystery out just like you have."

"What?" she stumbled.

"I'm not really a doctor, though fortunately, I've had some training. Frank?"

A man walked out. "This is Frank, the real doctor here. I've been undercover for a few weeks to catch the killer, and you've been a great help."

Frank went back to where he had come from and all Susan could think about was being in the dark again. Did Henry know?

"Susan." The words were calm. Henry looked into her eyes and as her own body shuddered, she couldn't help feeling like a fool. She'd come in search of a killer only to discover once again she'd been a pawn. Well, *she wouldn't do it again*, she thought, staring at the man she thought she loved.

"I didn't know either. I didn't know Charles here was undercover."

"Serious?"

The fake doctor nodded.

"I was in the dark as you and only discovered the identity of Charles here through the fist fight with the captain."

Susan was surprised, but remained unconvinced. "So, how did you manage to talk to him while you were fighting, huh?"

Henry giggled, then held his middle. "I sort of got him to the wall," Henry said. "My heart was killing me, I felt as if I was going to be sick..."

"Was there another fish?..."

"No, silly. My heart condition."

"Oh, Henry!" She wrapped her arms around him. He winced.

"Look," said Charles. "The captain has been running this ring for some time, but we could never prove it. I had to buddy up with him and hope he'd open up. He never did. But I watched him and started putting two and two together."

"So who killed Mr. McLean?"

"The captain, to keep him quiet. When Mr. McLean, his old friend, came to him with the goings on of the ship, including stolen jewels and a changed wife, Captain Starling knew his friend was here for more than just a honeymoon and he couldn't allow him to snoop around. He went to McLean's wife, hoping she could calm her husband and lessen his worry about both evils, only when he spoke with her, the captain noticed right away it wasn't Mrs. McLean but a young woman dressed up as his friend's wife. But that isn't everything."

Susan stood still, waiting, her arm still wrapped around Henry's waist.

"The captain knew right away of the farce, because he recognized the woman in the old woman getup."

"Rose," Susan said.

"He knew Rose and liked the control he held over her."

"You mean..." said Susan.

"That's exactly what I mean," said Charles. "And I'm sorry to say his indiscretions finally led to his downfall."

"What?" Henry gasped.

"Mrs. McLean and her granddaughter had a grand scheme going to pilfer money from old men, but it couldn't be hidden forever. And when the captain found out, he just added the new wealth to the accumulating wealth from the islands."

Suddenly Susan remembered something. "But what about your rough hands? I noticed their roughness when I faked being sick. Well?"

Charles blushed. "I do a bit of woodworking on the side." He walked over to a drawer and pulled out a lion, an ostrich, and a bear.

They were small enough to fit into the palm of his hand. "I go out searching, you know, when I can, for wood, and I do this on the side. It helps on those late nights when I have to stay up and follow some character that needs following."

Henry nodded, but Susan wondered.

"So Rose was killed by the captain because she was going to tell all," said Henry.

"It started simply enough – just a few jewels in the beginning stolen from a few homes, just a few old men taken for all they had, but when the captain got wind of it, he said he was *in* or all of those involved would lose their jobs. I was pretty worried myself and played along as much as I dared until we had sufficient information. What you need to know about the captain is he loves control and the control of the ship was no longer satisfying him. He's a man of adventure, that's for sure."

"And where is he now?" Susan asked.

"I have my man on him," Charles said, directing them to the door.

"And where is that?" asked Susan. She could only imagine the difficulties being hand-cuffed inside the bridge. "Would they reach the port safely once and for all?"

But Charles was smiling. Don't worry, we have someone else on the bridge. The captain is in the storage hold where he belongs. We wanted to give him the same treatment Mr. McLean and Rose received, but decided to handcuff him near the food. The morgue wouldn't have worked, but we got him as close as we could."

Afterword

Three days later, Maverick was no worse for wear. A week later, after being checked and double-checked at the hospital, he was given a clean bill of health and sent to jail. Captain Starling ended his career as a cruise ship captain and was later sent to prison. Jacob and his fellow conspirators were given two to five years for jewel theft.

As for the amberjack, they indeed had a way of making people sick – especially since the captain himself knew the fish had been contaminated by eating toxins found on seaweed and corral. But the amberjack *un-doctored* only made people ill; death wasn't on the horizon unless one added the additional poison Mrs. McLean offered.

When Maverick bungled killing Rose – he had used the amberjack without the extra dose of poison, the captain took the killing into his own hands. Rose probably had considered she and the captain a couple, but the captain was using her. It was too easy to kill Rose and peg the death on Jacob. With the help of security, who'd received payments from him as well, everything was set.

The real Mrs. McLean was given a heavy sentence – let's just say she would be in prison until the end of her days. She finally admitted to police she'd made millions marrying men for their money and then killing them off slowly using dimethylmercury; an untraceable poison gathered fairly easily from less than honest relatives who were also making a percentage of the profit.

In the end, it was always her. Her granddaughter never took care of the nitty-gritty and that's how she liked it. She felt sorry for her granddaughter who was a good girl with a smothering mother who wanted to keep her under lock and key. And it didn't help that her dead husband's brother was a snoop.

Those who had died on board, other than Mr. McLean and Rose had come by it honestly, if you can call swimming in polluted waters or eating uncooked shellfish with a touch of bacterium an honest way to go.

Still, of all the antics on the *Aloha*, most of those involved seemed crazy and a bit loco moco. Keith Kealoha and Dorothy Levine attempted solemn looks when the final verdicts were given on the criminals. Even Susan's mother thought her mix-up in the happenings on board far above the ordinary, and something a good daughter would never be involved in.

But for Susan and her Henry, a display of their vows and a kiss on Kaanapali Beach in Maui said it all. Sure, they'd been through some rough waters, opened up some cruel secrets, taken some punches and had been clamped and shackled, but today was a new day fit for a new start, a new life free of mystery.

What could possibly happen?

Loco Moco Recipe

Ingredients:

1/4 pound ground beef (hamburger)
1 egg
Cooked Rice
Hot prepared gravy
Hot pepper sauce
Tomato ketchup
Soy Sauce

Preparation:

Form the ground beef into a patty. In a frying pan over medium-high heat, cook patty until cooked to your liking; remove from heat and set aside.

Fry egg (sunny-side up or over-easy) in the grease from the ground beef.

Assemble this dish by putting a bed of cooked rice in a large bowl, top with hamburger patty, fried egg, and 1 to 2 ladles of hot gravy. Add hot pepper sauce, ketchup, or soy sauce according to your preference.

Makes 1 serving for a very hungry person.

SUNNY SIDE-UP